NEWPORT HARBOR HOUSE

CINDY NICHOLS

CHAPTER ONE

This couldn't be the last summer at the beach house, could it? How could her brother and father even consider selling it?

Jen tried to push the thought out of her head, as she'd been doing every day since she got wind of this idea—apparently one they'd hatched at a family meeting without her.

She couldn't believe her father and her brother had actually discussed the possibility of selling the beach house that had been in their family for generations. Where they'd learned to swim, taught their own kids to swim, had family reunions, laughed and cried and swept out more sand than could possibly be on the beaches in all of California.

She'd called her brother as soon as she could, asking what the problem was. He had hemmed and hawed—it's too expensive, we don't want to chip in for the taxes, it's so old—all the usual excuses.

She probably shouldn't have accepted the design job

that had kept her from the meeting, but who knew selling the beach house was on the agenda? She certainly hadn't.

But the design job was big. So big that she'd hesitated to take it on at all, as she wasn't a professional designer. She'd worked in a design shop part time for years, helping people choose fabrics and referring them to other designers. She'd learned quite a lot and had practiced mostly on her own house, and she'd only recently acquiesced to friends asking her to help.

While her father and brother had plotted against her, she'd spent hours working with delivery people and hanging the custom-made curtains that she'd designed.

This particular friend had been thrilled, but Jen wasn't sure the cost had been worth it—since she'd missed the meeting.

Their mother had left the house to all three of them —her dad, her brother and herself. It was clear that it had to be a joint decision between them to sell. And the decision, as far as Jen was concerned, was far from unanimous.

She hadn't quite given up hope yet. As the one who coordinated the calendar, she was pretty much in charge of the house. She had a few tricks up her sleeve to get her brother and her father to settle down, and she was looking forward to the summer to implement her plans.

She turned and looked around her garage one last time. Everything she thought she might need to do the minor repairs that had come up as an issue—paint, brushes, hammers and nails, along with rolls of fabric— was packed in the car. With as much renovating as she'd done to her own house, surely she'd be up to the task.

And she had help—Faith and Carrie were always up for an interesting project.

The beach house was her creative place, her happy place. She'd been going every summer since she was a kid. She couldn't wait to wiggle her toes in the sand and feel the cool breeze, sit on the deck and enjoy a glass of wine at sunset. With nobody to worry about but herself, enjoying the company of her two best friends. It was tradition. One she intended to keep.

At least she could look forward to that as soon as she got the puppy back inside after her disappearing act.

"Daisy. Daisy!" Jen stood at the open gate, her hands on her hips. Of all the times for the puppy to escape. It wouldn't be long before Faith arrived and they headed out on vacation.

"I should have known better." Jen turned toward the house, hoping Daisy would come right back and Jen wouldn't spend hours hunting her down. She and her son Max had tried to train her not to go out the gate and had had some success—apparently just enough to be lulled into the thought that she might not escape. And when she did, it was always at the worst time possible.

She kept an eye on the gate as she loaded up the bags of groceries—she'd stocked up on wine, and everything to make their traditional artichoke dip to enjoy on the deck at sunset later that evening was ready to go. She'd even brought new recipes to try over the summer. She loved to cook and her two friends were always willing to be guinea pigs.

After a couple trips to the gate and calls for Daisy, she was ready to load the last bits. As soon as she'd opened up the back door of the car to load it up, Daisy sped past her, hopped inside, laid down in the back seat and promptly took to licking her black and white fur.

"Oh, thank goodness. Don't get too comfortable in there, Daisy," Jen said as two big, blue eyes followed her every move. "You're not coming."

She scooted a bowl of kibble out of the way and loaded her remaining things in the back of the car.

"I think we're done, Daisy. You can get out now," Jen said absently. She looked around the garage, rummaging in the pockets of her jeans for the list she always had. She'd been making lists for at least twenty years. There was no other way to survive being a single mom to two boys—well, young men now—and trying to make a living. She plucked her reading glasses from on top of her head and looked over the items, reaching up on some of the higher shelves in the garage for her favorite beach chairs.

Just as she threw the last of the packed ice chests in the back of her car, a trickle of sweat ran down Jen's neck. The sooner she got to the beach, the better. In the cool ocean breeze, she could relax and take some much-needed time to go through her mother's things, pack them up and give the beach house some TLC.

It was big, lovely and right on the beach, but very old. It had been built many years before, one of the first on the harbor in Newport Beach, by her grandparents. Even then, the summer heat inland in California had been too much to handle, and land even at the beach was cheap in those days.

After years of being too busy to work on it and with the threat of it being sold, it was time for some sprucing up. She wasn't quite sure what she might find if she looked a little harder, after years of deferred maintenance. She grabbed her paint chips, painting supplies and house design magazines and threw them on the empty side of the back seat.

After a glance at her watch, she stepped up her pace. Faith would be arriving any minute—in fact, she was late —and they'd have to hurry to be on the deck to watch the sunset. As she took a last peek at her list, that familiar summertime excitement began to build in her chest and she was anxious to get on the road. She made one more pass through her house before she locked up, closing curtains and locking doors.

It was finally time. She'd been waiting for this for months—actually for years, as there wouldn't be any kids to chase around—and now that the time had come, she could barely wait any longer.

CHAPTER TWO

Faith put the finishing touches on the bulletin board in her classroom, carefully placing the students' names down the left side in colorful construction paper. She cleaned up the little pieces that had fallen to the floor and placed the scissors carefully back where they belonged. She looked around the classroom—the one she'd been in for the past ten years—and sighed.

Leaving behind the familiar scents of paste, finger paint and the basil plant her first grade class had lovingly grown from seeds—after a little extra water until she returned—she turned toward the door. She was ready.

She slipped the keys to her classroom into her pocket and closed the door behind her. Faith had spent the last week getting ready for the student teacher she'd be training—making duplicate lesson plans, getting all the supplies she needed from the workroom. After over twenty years of teaching, she knew the routine.

A tingle flitted through her as she became more

excited about this assignment, although she'd hesitated to take it. Her last summer's intern had been a little challenging, and by the end of summer school Faith had felt like a wet noodle. Student teachers, in her experience, were full of enthusiasm and new ideas and wanted to try out everything they'd learned from books in the classroom setting. And Faith did her best to accommodate them—but she had decades of trial and error under her belt, and she knew what kinds of things worked and definitely knew what wouldn't.

Her job for the summer, though, was to sit back, give her student teacher as much room to roam as she could and be there to right the ship when things didn't work out. That was why she was so excited about this assignment her principal, Amy, had offered her this summer. This particular teacher was assigned to summer school after her first full year, and their principal had asked Faith to supervise her a couple of days a week rather than a full week all summer long. Faith had been thrilled. That meant she could earn some extra money, which she sorely needed—her not-so-friendly divorce had left her on her own—but spend the bulk of each week down at the beach house with Jen and Carrie. It couldn't have worked out better.

She peeked into her classroom one last time and nodded, knowing she'd be ready for the first day of class. She had a week off before that started, though, and she intended to make the most of it, with her toes in the sand and a wine glass in her hand, watching the sunset.

Glancing at her watch, she realized how late she was.

Jen was likely pacing the driveway by now. She turned on her heel and bumped right into her principal.

"Oh, Amy, I'm so sorry. I didn't realize you were there."

Her principal smiled and nodded toward the classroom.

"No problem. Everything in order in there, as always?"

Faith smiled and nodded. "You bet. Ready for summer, Captain."

Amy laughed. "Thanks, Faith. I always know I can count on you, and I really appreciate that. Charity is lucky to have you, and I know you can—well, help her."

Faith paused and narrowed her eyes at Amy. She'd known Amy for many years and truth be told, Amy had been the best principal she'd ever worked for. And with that, she always knew when Amy was hedging.

"What is it that you're not telling me?"

Amy cleared her throat and took a quick glance at her shoes before she looked up, smiling.

"Nothing yet. Nothing at all. I'm meeting with her principal next week for lunch and I'll call you. How's that? I'm kind of doing this as a favor—you know, taking her on for the summer. I'll let you know how big a favor it is as soon as I find out, okay? Have a great week, and I'll talk to you soon."

Amy waved and flashed her a way-too-bright smile. Faith was confident that Amy would tell her the truth, let her know what she was in for, but with just what she'd heard so far, her tingle of excitement had turned into a sinking feeling in her stomach.

Her last stint with a student teacher had been an adventure, yes, but the one before that had been even more challenging. By the end of the summer, she'd felt as if all of her ideas were outdated, and that her years of experience really weren't appreciated. It had been a tough summer, and she'd vowed never to do it again. Reason enough to be thrilled about this summer's part-time assignment.

Nearing retirement, though, every penny counted, and she was hoping that if she worked enough summers, she might be able to retire early. Keeping that in mind, she vowed to just wait and see what Amy had to say next week, and in the meantime, she had a date to keep that involved wine, artichoke dip, the ocean and a sunset.

CHAPTER THREE

F aith couldn't help but roll her eyes as Jen tried to hold on to the collar of Max's new puppy when she came in the gate. Why her friend had acquiesced to Max's plea, Faith would never know. Sometimes she thought it was Jen's soft spot for dogs in general—though you'd never know from the look on her friend's face at the moment that she had any soft spot for dogs at all.

Faith wiped her hands on her jeans and grabbed a broom on her way. She looked up into the flittering leaves of the eucalyptus trees that dotted Jen's property, and she began to sweep as many as she could off of the driveway before they left. Jen always had so much work to do, as a single mom to two boys. Faith always tried to help when she could.

Her friend seemed to never stop. Faith looked up at the beautiful, two-story house that Jen and her husband Allen had built with their own hands so many years ago. Jen was constantly changing something—new curtains, new tile, even re-arranging furniture, and it looked like it was out of a magazine. Jen truly had a gift for design. But lots of times, Faith got tired just thinking about all that change.

"I don't know why we even keep trying to clean all these leaves. As many fall as we sweep," Faith said with a smile. "And we're leaving."

"I know. Futile. But they're there, so I have to do it."

Faith nodded and took her bags over to Jen's car, wiping the perspiration from her forehead after she got them inside.

"Boy, it sure is hot all of a sudden. Perfect time to leave. Thanks for asking me to come with."

"Don't be silly. It wouldn't be the same without you. We've done this every summer for how long—decades?"

Faith reached into her car for her purse and sunglasses. "Yep, about that long. Mostly just weekends for me, though. Since the kids were babies. But I have to say, I was really worried that after your mom—well, that you all might decide to sell it. It's probably worth a fortune."

Jen paused for a moment as she tossed the leaves in the dustpan into the trash.

"I'm a little worried about that, too. They had a big meeting around Easter, and my dad said there was nothing really to talk about, but I don't buy it. I know they don't want to put any big money into the house, but hopefully I can do enough little things to make it look better. Or newer. Or something."

Faith smiled. The house was old, granted, but it had a quaint, lived-in feel even if it was outdated.

"How does the calendar look for this summer?" It was a given that Jen's brother's family might come and go, but Faith didn't mind. There was plenty of room, and now that she thought about it, they hadn't come down much in recent years.

"I called my brother to see who wanted to book for which weeks this summer, and nobody wanted to. Not even his kids. Not sure what's going on. But for now, we just get to spruce it up, pack up some of Nana's stuff and just enjoy the weather. The cooler weather."

"Well, that's a relief. I've been looking forward to it for months. I couldn't wait for school to get out."

"Same here," Jen said. "I can't believe it'll be our first time without any kids. None at all, except for weekends, maybe. I'm sorry you can't stay for the whole summer."

"I agree completely. Wish I could have stayed the whole time. But you know how it is. Saving up for retirement."

"I know. Much as you love it, it must be getting old," Jen said.

Faith laughed. "Definitely. And I'm getting old, too. At least it feels that way."

"Nah, not yet. We're in the prime of our lives. Fifty is the new thirty—or so they say. And all the kids are up and out. Everything's going well. We get to just enjoy."

Jen cocked her head toward Faith. "I thought we might be seeing Maggy, at least occasionally."

Faith's daughter Maggy worked in San Diego, and while they were close—at least most of the time— Maggy had a pretty big job and couldn't get away too often. "Oh, right. Yes, she may stop in for a weekend or two, if that's all right. She'll be busy at work mostly, though."

Jen shook her head. "No problem. Wish we could get Max to come, too. Maybe for a weekend or something."

Faith sighed. "We've been trying to fix them up almost since the day they were born. I don't think this summer's going to be any different."

Faith's daughter Maggy and Jen's son Max had grown up together and spent their summers in Newport as well. They'd always harbored a not-so-secret hope that the two would end up together, but it never had worked out.

Faith leaned against the car. "I guess you're right. Hope springs eternal, though. I guess it's going to be just us, and hopefully we'll be able to talk Carrie into taking some time off. She said she would."

"That'd be great. Even a dentist needs a break every once in a while, I'm sure."

"Looks like we've got enough food." Faith put her last bag of groceries in the back. "Maybe we brought too much. It's not like there aren't stores in Newport."

"I know. But we always do this—at least I have plans for things I've been wanting to make. So I'm ready. I've been collecting recipes for months, and all the odd things to go with them."

"Great." Faith took out a package of dried Egyptian dates and turned it over in her hand. "And I'm ready to be your test-taster," she said with a laugh.

"Good. I should put a welcome sign for guinea pigs in the kitchen." Jen took a last peek in the bags they'd loaded. "I don't see any donuts. I thought you were going to bring them."

Faith looked in the bags and shrugged her shoulders. "Guess I forgot. Besides, we'll have Nana's muffins." Jen glanced at Faith.

"Of course, we'll still have to go to the bakery by the pier," Faith said with a smile.

Faith felt her friends' eyes on her and knew she was smiling, but she looked away. She was never very good at hiding anything.

"That wouldn't have anything to do with the older Mr. Johnson retiring last year and the younger Mr. Johnson taking over, would it?"

"Uh, no, why?" Faith asked.

"If I recall correctly, he gave you free donut holes every chance he got. Just like his dad did for my brother and me when we were little kids."

"Right. It's just a tradition. But they're great donut holes."

Jen laughed out loud at that one. "Yes, they are. And the cinnamon buns are pretty stellar, too." Faith couldn't believe she'd said that out loud, and felt heat creep up her neck.

Fortunately, Jen's phone rang, and Faith took the broom Jen handed her and continued sweeping.

"Hi, Max," Jen said to her younger son. "How did the final meeting go for your internship?"

Faith's ears perked up. Max had just graduated from college and had applied for internships across the country as well as in their hometown. This last interview was a long shot—and in Boston. But it was the best of the internships available, and Faith was rooting for him.

Faith kept sweeping, purposefully heading in a

different direction than Jen so she didn't eavesdrop. Not that she wouldn't have liked to.

Jen walked back in her direction with her arms folded and her brows furrowed. Faith leaned the broom against the wall of the house and took in a deep breath.

"What happened? He didn't get it?"

Jen leaned back against the hood of her car, her arms still folded, shaking her head. "Worse. He did."

"Oh," Faith said slowly as she looked up at Jen's big house and around at all the leaves. If Max was heading to Boston for the summer, she'd have to make arrangements for somebody to check on the house. "Maybe Michael could come and look in on the place?"

Jen's older son, recently married, was living in a tiny apartment closer to town, but he probably wouldn't mind.

"That's not the problem," Jen said.

Faith's eyes followed Jen's as she looked toward the back seat of the car. The cute little puppy raised its head and stood up, and its tail thudded on the seats faster than Faith had ever seen.

"Ah, I see."

She walked over to the car and patted her friend on the shoulder on her way. "It'll be all right," she said as Jen opened the back door and added the big bag of dog food.

"Guess you're going on our trip with us, Daisy. You ready?"

CHAPTER FOUR

C arrie Westland said goodbye to her last patient of the day—Mrs. Thurston, of the Laguna Thurstons, whose teeth sparkled in the sunlight —and hung up her white coat on the back of her office door. She rubbed her hands together with sanitizer and watched out the window as Mrs. Thurston—the second or third wife of Randall Thurston—tried to navigate the concrete of the parking lot in her six-inch heels. In the middle of the afternoon. In the summer.

She shook her head and called to her receptionist. She'd asked that Andrea make no appointments for the afternoon as Jen and Faith would be arriving, and they needed to perform their ritual inauguration to the summer. Sitting on Jen's deck and watching the sunset— and passersby—had become a tradition over the years, and she had no intention of missing it.

"Is that it? Nobody else today?"

"That's it," Andrea said from the front desk. "This is always my favorite holiday."

Carrie laughed as her receptionist perked up, turned off the computer and reached for her purse. It was a sort of holiday, she supposed. At least for her, and by trickle-down for her staff. She worked hard, and her staff was as dedicated as she was, so it was nice that they could take some time off and enjoy the early summer in Newport.

"Great. Enjoy. You heading to the beach?" Carrie asked.

"You bet. Wouldn't miss it. The tourists will be descending like locusts before too long. Gotta catch as many waves as we can before then."

Andrea's boyfriend was a champion surfer, and although he spent much of his time surfing around the world, he and Andrea still loved to catch the local waves. While they could.

"Okay, be careful. See you Monday."

"Thanks, Dr. Carrie," Andrea said, already halfway out the door. Carrie wondered for a moment if she already had her bathing suit on underneath her scrubs. It wouldn't surprise her.

"Oh, wait. This guy called three times today. And it's only a half day." She handed three pink message sheets to Carrie.

Carrie glanced at the messages—Dirk Crabtree. Again.

"Thanks," she said as she dropped them into her pocket.

Andrea looked from the trash can to her boss. "Not going to call him back, huh? He's been calling for weeks."

Carrie shook her head. "Nope. Not interested in what

he has to say. Go ahead and get going. I'll make sure he stops calling."

"Okay, thanks—I think," Andrea said. She took a quizzical look back at her boss before the door slowly closed behind her.

"You're welcome, and don't forget your sunscreen!"

Andrea held up a bottle and waved as she got into her Volkswagen van, her surfboard sticking out the back.

Carrie turned back into the office and glanced around. It was a small office, but she liked it that way. Offers to work at the bigger clinics had come regularly through the years, but she'd always said no. She liked working on the small side, and somehow she'd built a pretty big practice. Once people like the Thurstons had found her, anyway, and that was probably thanks to her mother.

She'd never once asked her parents for help, but as her parents were heavily involved in fundraising for the hospital and the yacht club, she was pretty sure they'd thrown their daughter's name into the pool. Life was good—if that Crabtree guy would just leave her alone.

She glanced at her watch, figuring she had just about enough time to go home, change her clothes, grab a bottle of wine and walk up the beach to Jen's house. Well, not Jen's house exactly but the Watson family house. She wondered a bit how it was that Jen had it for the whole summer, and neither her brother nor his kids would be coming. She was sure she'd hear all about it later.

She considered stopping at the farmers' market for something to take—an appetizer, maybe—but shrugged it off. Everybody knew she didn't cook and pretty much no longer expected her to. Besides, Jen and Faith always had artichoke dip on their first night, and there was enough for an army.

She pulled out of the parking lot, the top of her convertible down. It was still cool enough, with the Fourth of July still a bit away, and she tugged on the wide-brimmed hat that she kept on the front seat. Faith and Jen had told her she looked silly, but there was no way she was going to risk early wrinkles or skin cancer, so the hat had become her go-to.

She turned onto the Balboa Peninsula and headed down Newport Boulevard, past the restaurants, docks and all kinds of houses that would soon be filled with summer renters. For now, the roads were mercilessly free of people and small children trying to run as fast as they could to stake their claim on the beach, but she drove carefully anyway.

Pulling into the garage of her townhouse, she carefully weaved through the golf clubs, tennis rackets and beach umbrellas and dropped her purse onto the white marble kitchen island. The ocean breeze blew in the sliding glass doors, and Carrie took in a deep breath. Even though she'd lived in Newport her whole life, she never took for granted the sand, the sun, the breeze—all of it.

She peered into her wine cooler and picked out a Pinot Grigio she knew the girls would love. She opened her refrigerator, somehow thinking that an appetizer might have magically appeared that she could take—but it hadn't. It was basically empty but for some hard-boiled eggs, half-and-half for her coffee and a container of peanut butter.

Her phone buzzed in her purse, and she smiled at the name on it—Jen.

"Hey! You guys here already?" she asked.

"Hi, Carrie," she heard in the background.

"Hi, Faith," she answered, as Jen said, "Nope. Getting a little bit of a late start. Sorry. We had some unexpected last-minute changes."

"Oh, no. Everything okay?" Carrie thought she heard a bark, but that couldn't be.

Jen sounded annoyed. "Yes, everything's fine. Or I hope it will be. I'll text when we get there. Can't wait to see you."

"Same. I'll be ready."

Carrie clicked off, and paced once or twice around the couch, not sure what to do with her nervous energy. It'd take the girls at least an hour to get there, maybe more with traffic. California traffic had only gotten worse in the last few years, and Carrie thanked her lucky stars that she got to stay put right in Newport, year-round.

She glanced at the crumpled messages from Dirk Crabtree on the table. She wasn't sure who he was, but she was absolutely sure he was calling because of her mother. Nobody was that persistent unless her mother had put him up to it.

The name was vaguely familiar, but she couldn't quite place it—whether from the yacht club or the hospital board, she didn't know. Clearly he wasn't someone who'd left an impression on her, or she'd remember.

The phone number was local but someone who called

that frequently but didn't leave a message—well, maybe her mother would spill if she'd been involved in any way.

Her phone rang, and she picked it up, wrinkling her nose when she looked at the caller ID.

"Hello, sweetheart," her mother said when she answered her phone. "How are you?"

The sticky sweet voice on the other end of the line told Carrie all she needed to know. Usually, her mother was quick and to the point—unless she wanted something.

"Hello, Mother." Carrie plopped down on the couch, ready for it to take some time for her mother to get to the point. "I'm fine. Waiting for Jen and Faith to get here. It's the start of summer."

She literally heard her mother sniff before she commented. "So it is. For some of you, I suppose."

"Yes, it is, and I'm excited. What's up?" Carrie always tried to keep it light—and fast.

Her mother cleared her throat, then continued. "I suppose if those friends of yours are coming into town, you wouldn't be available for dinner tomorrow night. There's someone I'd like you to meet."

Ah, there it was.

"No, I'll be busy this weekend, for sure. Likely every weekend this summer. Jen and Faith get to stay the whole summer. It's going to be great."

"Hm, I'm sure it will be."

Carrie almost laughed at her mother's sarcasm. No point calling her on it, though. She'd learned over the years that didn't end well.

"Yes, it will be."

After an awkward silence, her mother said, "Well, I have a favor to ask you."

Carrie stood and took in a breath. Her mother's picks for her were horrific and the dates were excruciatingly endless.

"Oh?" Carrie asked, her fingers crossed for good luck.

"Yes, dear. As you know, I am chairman of the fundraising for the hospital board. The hospital you refuse to work at."

Carrie sat down hard. "Mother, you know I love my clinic. The hospital doesn't have dentists, anyway."

"Oh, right. You decided to be a dentist, after all that training. You could have been anything, you know."

Carrie did, in fact, know that she could have chosen any specialty at all, but she'd thought long and hard about what she wanted to do, and dentistry had somehow caught her fancy. It had helped that the man she'd fallen in love with was also a dentist, and they'd opened a clinic together. But her mother knew all that and still liked to needle her.

"Yes, I know. So what do you need from me? About the hospital?"

Her mother cleared her throat again. "Now, don't say no right away. Just think about it."

"Think about what?" Carrie paced in front of the mantel, glancing at a picture of her mother and herself from long ago. Neither of them was smiling, she noticed, not for the first time.

"Maude will not be able to serve as my donations coordinator for the Labor Day benefit. I'd like you to do it."

Well, there it was. Maude and her mother had been cohorts for decades, and Carrie had fortunately been left mostly out of the loop, except for her expected attendance at said events. This was a disaster.

"Oh, no. What's happened to Maude?" Carrie asked, legitimately concerned for more reasons than one.

"It doesn't matter. What matters is that I need help and you are my daughter."

Maude was a dear friend of her mother's—or so Carrie had thought—and she did hope that the older lady was all right as she wondered what had happened. She paused, trying to formulate her next question.

Her mother didn't wait long. "Carrie, I need you. I'll check in with you later so that we can start planning."

Her mother clicked off and Carrie glanced out the glass doors toward the waves crashing against the beach. Not for the first time, she felt pulled by the tides—truly wanting to help her mother and wondering why it was always so difficult. A fundraiser was no small thing to put together, especially with a hospital this size, and she didn't know a thing about fancy parties. She could barely get the right clothes together to even go, let alone plan.

Her phone dinged with a text from Jen.

We're almost there. Made great time. Come over.

Carrie's mood lifted, and she took another glance at the picture on her mantel—right next to the one with Carrie and Bethany. Carrie and her stepdaughter both *were* smiling, and even though Carrie hadn't seen Bethany a ton since Carrie had divorced Bethany's father, she and Bethany had had many happy times together, which she couldn't say about her own mother. She shook her head and decided to shelve the entire subject for later.

Be right there, she texted in return, a smile back on her face.

She ran upstairs and opened her closet, hopping into plaid walking shorts and pulling on a neon orange t-shirt and visor. She opened the sliding glass door to her upstairs deck, breathing the sea air again. Up and down the beach people strolled as others roller-skated along the boardwalk.

"Yep, summer has officially arrived," she said out loud before she headed downstairs to grab the wine and hang out with her best friends.

CHAPTER FIVE

The streets of Newport were crowded, even for this early in the season. Thank goodness her grandparents had built a garage during the original construction. There were lots of times that there was nowhere else to park.

Faith hopped out and hoisted the old, wooden door so Jen could pull the car in. They gingerly opened the car doors, trying not to hit the doors on the walls.

Jen maneuvered carefully around the car so as not to knock anything off of the shelves that brimmed full with surfboards, beach umbrellas, chairs and boogie boards. Snorkels and fins filled a cupboard, along with plastic shovels and buckets that the kids had used endlessly over the years to build their sandcastles.

"Guess we won't be using a lot of this stuff this year, huh, with the kids not here?" Faith asked as they carefully wiggled between the car and the shelves.

Jen glanced wistfully at the shelves of kids' toys. The prospect of spending time on her own with her friends was alluring, but she looked forward to the day when she might have grandchildren and start the cycle all over again. Little ones running around with sandy feet, learning to swim, sandcastles on the beach, frozen bananas at the Fun Zone. She might even go on the Ferris wheel just for fun. She missed it all.

"I don't know. Maybe we'll have grandkids and we can do it all over again."

Faith paused and picked up an empty bucket with colorful seashells on the side.

"I hope so. I remember it all so vividly. It'd be fun to have some babies running around, wouldn't it?"

Jen nodded. "Yes. But for now, maybe we'll have our own sandcastle contest. And I think we should definitely get out the paddle boards, don't you?"

"Oh, right, I forgot about those. I haven't been working out much. Haven't even had time to go walking. It'll probably kill me. I might be better off in a kayak," Faith responded. "I'm sure I can use Carrie's."

"Suit yourself. But I think we should try anyway. We can take them on the bay side where there are no waves."

The Newport house was uniquely situated so that it had pretty close access to the bay as well as being on the beach. There were only a few houses like that, and Jen always been grateful that her grandparents had taken a prime spot before they decided to build.

Faith leaned out of the garage door and looked up and down the street.

"Look at that," she said, pointing south.

"What?" Jen asked as she followed her friend out the garage door, following the direction she was pointing in.

She whistled, long and slow. "Wow. That wasn't here last summer."

Her hand shielding her eyes from the sun, Jen stared at what had been one of the last empty lots on the street. No one could ever figure out why it hadn't sold before now, but it had been a handy throughway from the beach to the bay side for most people.

"Guess we won't be going that way to the boardwalk anymore," Faith said.

The huge, modern house crept out onto the beach side and blocked their view south to the bay. It was mostly glass—and would have spectacular views—but that view would go both ways.

"I can't imagine living in a house like that. At night it'd be like a fishbowl. You can see just about everything."

"Guess that's the style now," Jen said, knowing full well it was. Newport had changed a lot over the last couple of decades, with people buying the old, traditional cottages and either completely gutting them or tearing them down altogether. This one was new—and to her mind, not very pretty. They'd even cleared out the grove of cedar trees that had dotted the property.

"I guess so, but it's—I don't know."

"I know what you mean." Jen knew exactly what her friend meant. As she turned back toward her family house, she noted that it was the last original left on their small street. It was quite large, by beach standards, with lots of bedrooms—though they were awfully small—and a very steep set of stairs to a small suite over the garage, which they called the studio.

The house still had the original windows, wooden

ones that stuck most of the time, and the wide, wooden porch had been re-stained more times than Jen could count. They hadn't had lots of money to fix it up—and her brother didn't seem to want to do anything differently now—but Jen had always spent her summers giving it as much TLC as she could.

Her grandmother, Nana, had lived there the last couple of decades before she passed away, and it was part of the charm of coming—Nana's muffins had no rival, and the sweet smell of them baking was part of the warm and fuzzy memories Jen had stashed away.

Jen maneuvered through the crowded garage toward the door. It took more than one tug to open it, and Daisy raced through into the small, fenced courtyard, almost knocking both Jen and Faith over in her hurry to get to the small patch of grass.

Faith followed Jen up the creaky steps, her arms full of grocery bags. She set them down on the porch as Jen fumbled with a ring of keys.

Jen flipped the keys around several times, found the right one and slipped it into the lock. She turned it several times, holding the knob firm with one hand as she'd always done in the past.

"It doesn't seem to want to open," she said finally, looking up at the porch awning, sun pouring through places it shouldn't be.

"Let me give it a try." Faith jiggled the key in the lock. "Hm. It seems to be stuck," she said with a grimace. "You sure it's the right key?"

Jen nodded and walked to the other side of the deck. Seagulls called from the beach, and the warm breeze and smell of the sea spray begged her to sit. But they had to figure out how to get in the house first.

"It must have rusted shut since anyone was here last. I'm sure somebody would have told me."

"Seems so. I'll go check in the garage for some WD-40. That takes care of anything."

Faith came back with the familiar blue can and sprayed around the door handle. "Maybe that'll do it."

Jen wiggled the key in the lock again and shook her head.

"Nope. We need a Plan B."

"All right. Maybe a window's open."

"Shouldn't be, but I guess it's our best bet."

Daisy raised an eyebrow from her resting spot on the small plot of grass in the courtyard as Faith and Jen circled the house, trying each window. The windows were quite old, but proved to be very sturdy, unfortunately.

With one last side of the house to try, they exchanged glances. The gate to access the south side of the house had been long rusted shut—and on the long list of fixes Jen had planned to get to this summer. But that was where the back door was, and it was their only hope.

Jen looked up at the second story. "If we can't get that last window open, we're going to need a ladder."

"Right, but one of us is going to have to hop the gate to get over there."

"Right," Jen said as they exchanged glances again. Neither one of them had been working out much beyond walking, and the six-foot fence had spikes at the top.

Jen had pulled her shoulder the previous spring and

had tried not to do too much heavy lifting while it healed, and Faith knew it.

"Okay, I'm on it."

After a bit of a struggle, Faith got to the top of the gate and swung a leg over, trying to scoot over the top of the gate without getting tangled up on the spikes.

"Thanks, Faith," Jen said, trying to keep her laugh out of her voice.

"Don't thank me yet." Faith looked down from the top of the fence, looking as if she was trying to get her courage to jump. "I still have to get to the bottom. And there's no guarantee we can open this door, anyway."

"Well, I've got a cold glass of wine for you when you meet with success."

Faith nodded. "Okay. I'll hold you to it." Faith turned around, her voice a whisper. "There's somebody watching me from next door. I can see the curtain twitching."

Jen shook her head. "That's just Mrs. Grover. A curtain-twitcher from way back. She's harmless, although she does seem very interested in whatever we do over here."

Faith too another glance in the direction of Mrs. Grover. "Okay. I'm going in, then."

Jen stiffened as Faith took a deep breath and disappeared on the other side of the gate. She held her breath for a moment, relieved she heard a deep belly laugh rather than a screech.

"Oh, my goodness," Faith finally said when she caught her breath.

"What?" Faith couldn't see through the wooden gate.

"Nothing. I'll show you in a minute. I'm going to try the door."

Jen listened as the keys jingled.

"Success!" Faith shouted, and Jen ran back around to the front of the house.

Faith swung the door open wide, a smile plastered on her face and her jeans ripped all the way across the back.

"Oh, my gosh." Jen held her stomach as Faith spun around, the back pocket of her jeans ripped down to show her pink-flowered underwear.

"It got caught on the spike, but I was already on my downward trajectory," Faith said, a giggle escaping as she pulled her t-shirt lower over her hips.

"Oh, I'm so sorry. But you got us in!"

Faith nodded as Daisy came bounding through the front door and began to inspect her new location.

"Yep. It was worth it, and I'd do it again. And I'm ready for my reward."

Jen laughed and brought in some of the grocery bags. "Coming right up."

CHAPTER SIX

J en couldn't take her eyes off the puppy, who was sniffing every nook and cranny of the beach house. It made her a little nervous, as she obviously didn't know Daisy very well.

She paused with the corkscrew in her hand. "I think I'm going to take Daisy for a quick walk and I bet she'll take a nap after that," Jen said. "Wanna come?"

Faith stretched and glanced longingly at the beach. "I'd love to, but isn't Carrie going to be here any minute?"

"We can head along the beach in her direction and catch her. Daisy really needs to air out, anyway. Maybe we can get her to swim."

Faith laughed and nodded in agreement as Jen clipped the leash on Daisy and led her out the door.

Jen closed the garage door—mentally adding an electric garage door opener to her list—and they went around the side of the house, tossing their shoes on the steps of the porch.

"There's nothing quite like the feeling of the sand in my toes," Faith said. "I look forward to it every time."

Jen wiggled her own toes and Daisy sniffed at the sand, something new to her. The puppy stepped gingerly at first, and when her paws sunk a bit, she tested it again. Finally, she decided it was fun and pounced around, rolling in between the sea grass and sending a resting group of seagulls to flight.

"Looks like she'll enjoy her summer," Faith said as she caught up with her friend, who had been pulled toward the water faster than either of them had expected her to.

Daisy plunged into the waves, and Jen laughed at the puppy as she stopped dead short, then backed up with a bit of a whimper.

"It's okay, Daisy. It's just the ocean," Jen said, bending down and petting the dog with a reassuring nod. She couldn't take the leash off—there was a beach up the road that was a dog beach, where they could run free, but this wasn't it.

Jen tiptoed into the cool water, coaxing Daisy along with her. In a matter of seconds, Daisy was running in circles, patting at the water and trying to catch the droplets in her mouth.

Jen's feet dug into the warm sand as Daisy played, pulling the end of the leash over her wrist.

"Wow, she's a handful." Faith caught up with Jen on the shoreline and stopped running, her hands on her knees as she caught her breath.

"What was that you said? Two against one?"

Faith laughed. "Uh, yeah, but right now she's all yours."

As Daisy tired of her current game and raced up the beach toward another dog, Jen had to follow along. Daisy was stronger than she looked, and Jen held her big, floppy hat on tightly as they raced up the beach.

CHAPTER SEVEN

C arrie tucked the bottle of wine under her arm and headed down the beach. She started on the boardwalk, and felt around the brim of her hat, making sure that no skin was left exposed. She peered up at the sun—it was early afternoon, but the hottest part of the day. No sense risking a sunburn.

Even though Jen's house was only a few down the row, Carrie gravitated toward the waves, preferring to walk on the sand whenever she could. And it was always best to take advantage of a slightly empty beach—it would soon be covered with people and getting to the rippling tide would be a bit of a challenge.

She waved at people she knew as she walked. Having grown up not too much further down the beach, in her parents' massive house that overlooked both the beach and the harbor, she always saw familiar people on her walks. But she stopped short as a man close to her age approached, his head down as he studied the sand beneath his bare feet.

As they came closer together and she realized who he was, she knew she'd have to say something. She hadn't seen Joe Russo in years. Maybe even a decade. But his dark brown, wavy hair and his tall, thin line were unmistakable, even at a distance. She'd heard that he and his wife had divorced—the bridge club her mother had belonged to for almost fifty years made sure everyone heard. Something quite a while back, but she couldn't quite remember. He and his wife had moved away from Newport years ago, after Allen died, and she hadn't seen him since. She also knew—just in general, not from the bridge club—that his father had passed about a year prior, so she wasn't all that surprised to see him back. His father had run the biggest gondola company in Newport, and even the bridge club had been atwitter about who would run it. Or if they would sell.

"Hi, Joe," was all she could come up with. Carrie's mother could talk to anyone, anywhere, and make them feel like they were the only person in the world. She, on the other hand, had never been very good at awkward conversations.

Joe stopped and dug his toes a little deeper in the wet sand as he looked up, cocked his head and seemed to be trying to get his bearings.

"Carrie. Carrie Westland," she offered, hoping to jog his memory. Maybe his memory was as bad as Carrie's seemed to be getting these days.

He nodded, and a slow smile spread across his face. Carrie had always liked him, and was forever grateful that he and his wife had been so kind and helpful when Jen's husband had had his tragic accident. It would have been much harder—which was difficult to even imagine—without them.

He dropped the shells he'd been collecting in his pants pocket and quickly wiped the sand off before extending his hand.

"Hello, Carrie. So very nice to see you again. It's been a long time."

"It sure has. I can't even remember when—I mean, it really has been a long time." She wasn't even sure if she should ask how he'd been, his dad dying and all. She knew her mother would be cringing at her lack of manners if she were there, so she was grateful her mother was far, far away. She really wanted to tell him he should be wearing a hat, but it probably wasn't a good idea. "And it's nice to see you, too. I'm sorry about your dad."

His eyebrows rose, and his brown eyes clouded for a moment. He nodded again and looked out over the waves, his hand shielding his eyes. "Thank you. I miss him."

"I'm sure. He was a great guy. Everybody in Newport misses him." They stood silent for a moment, and Carrie wasn't sure what to say. She wasn't as skilled in dealing with awkward conversations as most doctors were, and she knew it. There wasn't that much bad news to deliver in her dental practice, except when young teenagers found out they'd be wearing braces for months. So she just waited, grateful that he eventually changed the subject.

"This beach sure is a sight for sore eyes."

Carrie looked out over the waves, and a few sailboats dotted the horizon

"Mm, I bet it is. How long are you here for? You taken out your boat yet?"

Carrie did remember that Joe and Allen had been a winning sailboat racing team when they were in school together, beating everyone else in the harbor. She'd lost to them once and given up the hobby—too much sun for her, anyway.

He pulled his gaze away from the boats and looked down at the sand. "No, not yet. I'm sure I'll get around to it. You still live up the beach?"

Carrie turned and looked toward her condo, pointing. "Yep, right there." She actually lived pretty close to Joe's mom, and assumed that was where he'd been staying. "How long you here for?"

He shoved his hands in his pockets.

"Not sure. For the summer, at least. Kind of re-grouping."

Joe's dog—a beautiful black lab—began to tug, and Joe gripped the leash tighter.

Carrie smiled and nodded. She looked past Joe, over his shoulder, as a woman with a floppy hat tried to keep up with a very energetic puppy—a cute one who looked like a border collie. The woman kind of looked like Jen, but it couldn't be. Jen didn't have a puppy.

The puppy crashed against the back of Joe, knocking him to his knees. He laughed as the puppy licked his face, her paws on his chest, covering him in flying sand.

"Oh, my gosh, I'm so sorry," the owner said, and Carrie laughed.

"Hi," Carrie said as she realized that it was, in fact, her dear friend.

Jen's eyes met Carrie's wide ones, and Carrie cocked her head down toward the man who was laughing while he tried to untangle the two dogs' leashes. He wasn't meeting with much success, and Jen leaned in to help him.

She bent down, unclasping her puppy's leash. She untangled the two dogs and put the leash back on, taking a few steps back and finally wrangling her puppy closer to her. The dog's tongue lolled to one side and her tail beat the sand, but she sat at Jen's feet.

"That's the first time I've gotten her to sit," Jen said as she wiped her brow. She smiled at Carrie, who again tilted her head toward the man. He knocked some of the sand from his dog while petting her, and finally got to his feet.

Jen looked at her questioningly, and Carrie had never wanted to be telepathic more than now to let Jen know who she'd just knocked over. She knew it would be a big surprise since they hadn't seen each other for decades. Jen finally followed Carrie's gaze and began to apologize, and as Joe looked up at the same time, they stood stock still, staring at each other.

———

Joe was frozen in place, and his feet wouldn't move an inch. He knew he should hug Jen, say hello, catch up, but he just couldn't. At least not more than a brief nod.

When he'd run into Carrie, he should have expected that Jen would be around. It was summer, and they were best friends, after all. But when he looked up from Boris after his wrestling match with the border collie, the surprise at seeing her face was overwhelming. He should have been better prepared.

He finally mustered a muted hello, and he found his voice well enough to thank her for the sympathies she'd given about Claudia's departure—he supposed everybody knew by now, and he'd reassured both Jen and Carrie that it had been a mutual decision and as it was years ago, the pain had passed.

But he hadn't seen Jen for years, if not decades, and seeing her now brought back the rush of his best friend Allen's passing—Jen's husband.

After some small talk, and an invitation to dinner which he declined—he explained that he wasn't quite up to peopling—he managed a smile, waved goodbye and turned up the beach toward his mother's house.

He walked past the small dunes in front, up the brick steps and sat on the stoop in front of the white, clapboard house that he'd grown up in. Boris sat by his feet and they both gazed out at the sailboats.

Memories swirled around him, unbidden. His father had taught him to sail almost before he could swim, and his love for the wind and water ran deep. His father had taught Allen, too, and they'd become his best crew, even winning some races together. But that was a long time ago.

When Carrie had asked if he'd been out on the boat and he'd said no, he didn't want to go into much more detail. He'd been out a couple of times with his dad when he visited, but somehow it had felt wrong without Allen—they'd both felt it.

It had been a tough few years and he'd come home to Newport to rest, help his mom go through his dad's things, make a decision about the family business, and try to get rid of memories. He hadn't anticipated—although he probably should have—that coming home wouldn't get rid of memories. It would only bring more.

CHAPTER EIGHT

J en looked back over her shoulder several times as she, Carrie and Daisy headed south toward the Newport house. Daisy did, too, but for probably a different reason.

"He looked good," Carrie said as she, too, looked back at Joe walking north toward his house. Boris was trotting alongside him slowly, and Joe took frequent glances toward the sailboats bobbing past the waves.

"He did, but oh, those sad eyes. It was like a dagger when I gave my condolences about his dad."

Carrie paused for a second. "I remember the same look in your eyes when Allen died. It was decades ago, but at the same time it feels like it was just last weekend. Things like that don't fade very quickly," Carrie said.

Jen remembered that Carrie had always told her that she looked like that, too. For an entire year after.

Jen shook off the memory. It was a long time ago, and things were very different now. "Too bad he didn't want to come over. I do know how he feels, but getting back in the world is the only remedy. Company would be good for him, and I'm sure Daisy would agree about Boris. One thing I learned is that it helps to talk about things. Reminisce. Remember the good stuff."

Carrie looked back one more time as Joe sat on the stoop, Boris plopping down beside him.

"Maybe he's just not ready yet," she said as they reached the Newport house.

The gate of the white picket fence creaked as Jen scooted Daisy inside and took off her leash. Jen brushed white paint chips from the gate on her now-dirty jeans and leaned back against it, looking up at the house.

"Ah, home sweet home. You happy to be back for another season?"

Jen shielded her eyes from the sun and looked up at the roof of the loft, the highest story. "Thrilled. But it looks as if home sweet home needs a little TLC. Faith'll have to tell you how hard it was to even get in here."

Carrie stomped sand off her feet before she climbed up the stairs. The wooden, weather-beaten door swung open, and she wrapped Faith in a big hug. It was her favorite time of year, and seeing her friends meant that summer had officially begun.

"Great to see you," Faith said. "I can't believe we're all together again."

Jen and Carrie followed Faith into the kitchen, where Carrie popped the bottle of wine into the freezer.

"I didn't know when you'd be back after I saw Daisy pull you up the beach, so I went ahead and made the artichoke dip."

Jen opened the oven and inhaled deeply. Artichoke dip was their inauguration tradition—tangy marinated artichoke hearts, parmesan cheese, cream cheese, onions —everything delicious. The creamy dip bubbled and had almost started to brown on the top, and in the sourdough bread bowl, it smelled divine. She couldn't wait to have some.

Dust plumed in the streaming sunlight as Jen took a stroll around the bottom floor of the house. Family pictures dotted the walnut-paneled walls and her grand-mother's collection of teapots sat on the yellow Formica counters.

Carrie plopped a stack of design magazines on the counter and looked around.

"It's too bad they've never let you remodel this place. Or redecorate, even. We could do wonders here," she said, holding up a magazine cover of a remodeled beach house up next to the orange and yellow flowered curtains that had to date back to the '70s. Maybe the '60's.

"It really is awful, isn't it? My mother always said, "Why bother when everything is always covered in sand?" And when the kids were little, it was still that way. Now that they're all grown up, maybe the others might agree to a little sprucing up here and there."

"Just in time for grandchildren to ruin it all," Carrie chimed in. She checked the bottle of wine and nodded, indicating it was cool enough. "I kind of like it the way it is. Brings back lots of memories. It wouldn't be the same without the orange and avocado chairs."

Jen laughed and fluffed an orange throw pillow with a tree embroidered on it in green yarn. "Yeah, I guess you're right. But we do need to attend to some of the deferred maintenance. We don't want the whole thing to actually fall down," she said, picking some white paint from the fence off of her jeans.

Carrie dropped a handful of bread cubes onto a baking sheet that Faith had handed her.

"Ah, I see you remember your job," Jen said. Carrie could barely boil water on her own, but she'd learned over the years how to be a good sous-chef—cutting up things for Jen and Faith to add to their trial recipes.

"Did Jen tell you that none of the family has booked time this summer?" Faith asked Carrie as she poured their glasses of the crisp chardonnay they'd brought.

Carrie raised her eyebrows as she turned to Jen. "No, she didn't. But it's not exactly like we had time for that. We ran into Joe."

Faith had been leaning toward the artichoke dip and stopped in mid-reach. She turned to Jen, her eyebrows arched. "Oh? How was that? We haven't seen him in —forever."

"I think I forgot to tell you that he and Claudia aren't together anymore. And his dad died. So we pretty much just said we were sorry for him, invited him over tonight, but he said no. And then came back."

"Oh, my gosh," Faith said, sitting slowly on one of the plastic orange bar stools. "I wish he would come. I'd love to see him. It's been a long time."

"Maybe he'll change his mind," Carrie said as the three of them loaded up a tray with the artichoke dip, a wine cooler with a fresh bottle in it and the bread to dip into the warm, creamy parmesan concoction.

Faith swung open the door to the main deck and the friends dusted off three orange cushions for the deck chairs, reached for their wine and toasted each other.

Jen lifted her glass toward the beach. "I hope so. But meantime, let's get this summer started."

CHAPTER NINE

The lasagna had been fantastic, as usual, just like Joe remembered. His mother had been in the kitchen all day, and he hadn't exaggerated when he'd told her it was probably her best ever.

Joe could feel his mother's eyes on him as they sat on the porch and watched the stars. He tried to ignore the nudge, but he figured that after fifty-odd years of her doing it, she wasn't going to change now.

"What's on your mind, Ma?" he finally asked, knowing she wanted to say something. When he'd come back from the beach, he'd told her he'd run into Jen and Carrie, and that they'd asked him over.

She, of course, had encouraged him to go, but he just hadn't felt like it. He imagined she had something to say about that, although they'd be winding down by now, he thought.

"Oh, nothing," she said. Which was what she always said—at first. This was also a game they'd played for a very long time, and although he'd been gone for quite a while, he still knew how to play. Some things never changed, and he was glad of it.

"Come on, I'm sure there's something on your mind. I can tell."

She set down her crossword puzzle and leaned forward in her rocking chair, looking down the beach.

"I can hear them laughing from here. Maybe you should go down after all. You can't just sit here and mope, you know."

There it was. He knew his mother had been worried about him since he'd come home. He'd been hesitant to tell her that he'd run into Jen and Carrie, expecting her to do exactly what she was doing. Encouraging him to get out. His mother was the one who'd just lost her husband —he should be worrying about her instead.

"I don't know. I'm happy here with you and Boris. Very peaceful," he said, leaning back in his beach chair as he sipped the last of his beer.

His mother let out a laugh. "Unless you want to give me a seven-letter word that means 'comparison' and help me finish this darned crossword puzzle, I'm not going to be much fun. You need to hang around with young people your own age. Not old folks like me. You need to get out."

He hadn't wanted to "get out" much before now, but he followed her gaze down the beach and he, too, could hear the girls laughing. He smiled at the sound—they'd all been such very good friends once upon a time.

But it had been a very long time, and the last time he saw them all, they were helping Jen adapt to her new life. He and Claudia had helped as much as they could, and once Jen seemed to be settled, they'd sort of gone their separate ways.

Then when he'd been offered the job in Chicago, they all promised to visit. But contact became more and more sparse, and eventually, he realized it had been years since he'd seen any of them.

Even when he visited his mother, there never seemed to be time to go out. Maybe he felt a little guilty about that—well, he did feel guilty about that. He should have checked in, asked how the boys were doing. Helped if he could. But he couldn't change any of that now.

But it had been a pleasant shock to see them today, even though he'd been stunned speechless. Jen probably thought he was upset about Claudia and while he had been when they'd first divorced, it had been a few years now and he felt like he was thawing out. He probably should go and apologize, actually, so she didn't think he was crying in his beer.

Joe reached down and stroked Boris's head. The sun had long set, and the stars were out in force. The cool breeze ruffled Boris's fur and his ears perked up at every seagull call and his tail thumped in a steady rhythm against the wooden deck.

His mother set the puzzle aside and went into the house, the wooden screen door snapping closed behind her. She came out in a second with a container in her hand—one he knew held her family's sauce recipe, handed down from generation to generation from Italy. He knew because there was always some in the freezer, just in case.

He never knew what the "just in case" his mother

always talked about was, but it dawned on him what it might be now.

She held out the container and nodded her head in the direction of Jen's house.

"Take it down there. They might be hungry."

"Mom, I suspect they might just be drinking wine and catching up. I don't want to interrupt."

His mother stiffened a bit and squared her shoulders. "Are you implying that your great-great-grandmother's sauce is an interruption?"

He noticed her sly smile before she turned back toward her crossword puzzle. He stood and stretched, reaching for Boris's leash, which had the dog at his knee in a flash.

"I guess I could take Boris for another walk. He doesn't seem quite tired enough yet."

His mother smiled and picked up her crossword puzzle, leaning back in her chair.

He started down the steps, turning back to his mother before he headed to the beach.

"Thanks, Mom. I know you're trying to help. And the word you're looking for is 'analogy'."

"Hm, you're right. Maybe you'd better stay after all," she said, peering over her reading glasses.

"Save the hard ones for me. I'll be back shortly, I'm sure."

———

Jen said goodbye to Carrie after offering to walk her home. Carrie waved her off and said she knew her way home just fine, thank you very much. Carrie patted Daisy on the head and said, "See you guys later," before she disappeared up the boardwalk.

Jen stood in the kitchen and stretched. Faith popped her head out of the stairwell and said, "I think I'm going to head up to the loft. Long day. I'll see you tomorrow. Maybe check my email, see if there's anything from Maggy."

"Night," Jen said, and she laughed as Faith poured herself another small glass of wine to take with her, wiggling her eyebrows as she headed up the stairs.

A loud creak stopped Faith in her tracks. She took a step back and gingerly put her foot on the step in question. It creaked again, and a chunk of the wood popped out, rolling down the stairs.

Daisy made straight for it, grabbing it in her mouth like a prize.

"Oops. Sorry," Faith said. She pulled a face to go along with her apology, and Jen took in a deep sigh.

"I guess we should add that to the list, too. Be careful on your way up. We can check out all the stairs in the morning."

Faith nodded and climbed the stairs slowly, her hand sliding gingerly up the rail.

Jen re-filled the bowls with food and water for Daisy, and she looked around for the puppy. She probably needed to go outside before she went to bed. The last thing she needed was doggy puddles around the living room, even if the carpet was horrible and had seen better days.

The puppy hopped off the couch when Jen called

her—tomorrow she'd have to start teaching her not to get on the furniture. Jen poured herself a small glass of wine and opened the door, sitting on the stoop as she pointed Daisy to the small patch of grass inside the white picket fence. While Daisy sniffed around, Jen sipped her wine. She leaned back, stars twinkling overhead like sparks of steel on black velvet, and let out a contented sigh.

"You always did love it here, didn't you?" she heard from beyond the gate. It was pretty dark with no moon, but she recognized Joe's voice instantly.

She leaned forward and smiled as he came into view under the streetlamp.

"Yes, this is true. My favorite place on Earth, I think."

He nodded and waved at Daisy.

"Mind some company for a minute? We didn't really get to have a proper conversation on the beach."

Jen stood, glad that he seemed to be in a friendlier mood. They'd all been such good friends once. She really didn't want to see him unhappy—and now he'd had his own challenges.

"Of course. Come on in. I'll grab you a beer."

He nodded in thanks and opened the creaky gate, raising his eyebrows. He let Boris off the leash to go play with Daisy and gratefully accepted the beer that Jen held out, exchanging it for the sauce his mom had sent.

"Your mom's sauce?" Jen's eyebrows rose in appreciation. "Wow, thanks."

Joe nodded and smiled before looking back at the creaky gate and up at the awning with a hole in it.

"Looks like the old house could use a good once-over," he said. He moved a brick to the side that had come out of the step. "Or maybe a ten times over."

"Apparently. I haven't been for a while. I knew there were big storms this year, but nobody mentioned we needed to do so much repair."

"Wind and weather are hard on beach houses, that's true," Joe said. "I haven't been at my mom's long, but there is the requisite list on the refrigerator that I'll need to get to as well. You're in good company."

Jen laughed and nodded.

They sat on the stoop and looked up as the stars continued to multiply in the black sky, the warm breeze making Jen feel like no time had passed at all—but of course it had.

"The girls are gone already? I was hoping to say hello and catch up a little bit. I'm afraid I was taken a bit off guard running into you guys on the beach, and I—I guess I didn't quite know what to say. It's awkward to talk about somebody dying, you know? And with divorce on top of that—well, it makes everybody uncomfortable."

Jen actually laughed and said, "Um, yes, I know. I know exactly."

He turned toward her with a horrified look on his face —again.

"Oh, my gosh, I'm sorry. I didn't mean that. Gosh."

He dropped his forehead into his hand, his elbow resting on his knee.

Jen laughed again. "Don't be sorry. It happens. A lot."

She patted his knee, hoping he'd lighten up a little bit. And it seemed to work. He looked at her and smiled.

"Thanks for that. It's just everybody gets so—I don't

know, stressed. It's been a while since Claudia and I divorced, and I'm really okay. Claudia and I had a good life before everything went south. It's really all right. And then my dad—"

Jen smiled at him—he really did seem okay.

"I suppose it gets easier with time."

Joe nodded and turned to look at Jen. "I see that. You look great. And my mom's caught me up a little bit, but I'd sure like to see how you are. I was sorry to hear about your mom passing, too. Shoot, there I go again."

Jen laughed and took a sip of wine. "Seems like there's no avoiding it. And I could say the same about your dad."

They both chuckled and nodded.

"So, how about everybody else? The boys—how are Michael and Max? Your brother, Greg. His kids. Your dad. Everybody good?" he asked, holding up both hands with his fingers crossed.

"Good job with that." She smiled as she pointed at his crossed fingers. "You're in luck. Everybody's fine. Michael is married, Max just graduated from college, Greg is—well, Greg is Greg."

Joe leaned back against the house and stretched his legs, his arms crossed. "Yes, I remember. Some things never change?"

Jen shook her head. "No, they don't. I don't see them much. Even less lately."

Joe let out a slow whistle. "Maybe for the best."

"Maybe," Jen replied with a nod. "I'm not really sure what's up. They usually still come out at least once a summer to stay here, but this year they're not."

Joe took the last sip of his beer. "No?"

"No. Kind of strange, but Carrie and Faith and I are thrilled we get it all to ourselves for the summer. Faith is teaching summer school but will be here every weekend. I have a couple of design jobs to do for friends, but they should be easy. Carrie's cutting back at her clinic, and we plan to kayak and walk—just relax. Oh, and fix up the house a little bit. Another beer?"

Joe held up his empty bottle and nodded. Jen reached in the kitchen and grabbed him another one.

"I was wondering about that. If Greg and Sylvia aren't using it, you going to sell the place? How will that work?"

Jen took in a deep breath. "I don't think anybody cares about it much. At least not right now. It's not costing them anything. Greg comes, but even that's not very often. They won't green-light any repairs, though, and as you can tell from the gate, the list of things that need fixing is pretty long. I haven't even had the chance to take a look around yet, but plan to first thing in the morning. Then Faith and I might go fabric shopping. I can pop for some new curtains, and nobody will be the wiser."

Joe leaned forward and peered in the windows. "Oh, wow, still the same orange and green ones?"

"Yep. Vintage 1970s. Only the best. And the shag carpet, too."

"Good grief. Well, I suppose it's practical, if not exactly appealing."

Jen tapped him lightly on the shoulder. "Hey, watch it. I love this place. I can't even imagine it with a total makeover. It would lose all its charm."

"Okay, whatever you say," Joe said as he snapped his fingers, and Boris came right over and sat at his feet.

"Wow, I think I might need you to be the puppy whisperer with Daisy. She doesn't know a thing. I'm not even sure she's housebroken," Jen said, then filled him in on how Daisy was even there to begin with.

Joe stood and stretched before clipping the leash to Boris's collar. "At your service, ma'am. And I'm happy to help with the house if you need me to. You know where to find me. My mom would be thrilled to see you, too. Stop by sometime."

"I will. Please tell her hello for me, and thank her for the sauce. It's like gold, so I'm especially grateful." She hadn't seen Joe's mom for years, and it would be nice to. "Thanks for stopping by," Jen said.

They both stopped at the faint sound of fireworks in the distance. They shared a quick glance and smiled.

"Disneyland fireworks. Like clockwork."

Joe nodded. "I can't believe you guys didn't stay up there long enough to watch from the deck. I find myself watching as much as I can."

Jen smiled. "We had an extra long day and I guess we forgot. We'll try to make it tomorrow."

"Remember all those times when we all snuck out and watched them from the roof? Allen was always game for that. And I think my dad actually knew anyway, even though he never said."

Jen looked in the direction of the sound. "I do remember. I was always afraid we'd get caught but we never did."

Joe shook his head. "There's no way the parents

didn't know what we were doing. Maybe they just wanted to let us see the magic anyway."

"Could be. So many memories like that," Jen said, looking slowly back at the house.

"Yeah. Lots of memories," Joe said as he headed toward the beach, and he waved just before he and Boris disappeared around the corner.

"All right, Daisy," Jen said as she opened the door for the new puppy. "Guess it's just you and me. Let's go get comfy. We've got the whole summer ahead of us."

CHAPTER TEN

J en slept like a log, the breeze billowing through the open windows and the waves lapping at the shore. Daisy had slept all night long, but as soon as the sun began to stream in, Daisy was up, too. Jen woke to a panting dog right in her face and knew from experience that it was in everybody's best interest for her to take the dog out right away.

They'd been at the beach house for almost a week, and they'd only had two accidents which weren't really Daisy's fault at all. Overall, she'd been a good influence, forcing regular walks on the beach morning and evening. Jen felt like she was even getting in a little better shape— walking on sand was tough on the legs, and she'd felt it for the first few days.

She checked the gate to make sure it was secure and let Daisy find her way around the patio to do what she needed to do. She waved at Mrs. Grover, who was looking out of her window, and Jen smiled when the older lady looked startled that Jen could see her. Jen was sure that she thought she was invisible, but there was no way to miss the twitching curtains. There'd been quite a bit of activity at the house the past few days, so Jen wasn't surprised she'd be curious.

She hadn't heard Faith stir yet, and glancing at the clock, Jen realized she might not see her friend for a while. She started the coffee, turned on the oven and took out the batter she'd made the night before for Nana's muffins. She'd called the basic recipe her "endless" muffins—a delicious white muffin base and she was always changing what she added to it. One day, it would be blueberries, another chocolate chips. Jen's personal favorite was cinnamon with crumbly topping, which was what she was making today.

Grabbing Nana's apron, she looped it over her neck and tied it behind her. Hands of Gold, it said in embroidery, and it was one of the things she remembered most about her grandmother—anything she cooked was fantastic, and she never cooked without her apron. Jen didn't think she was quite as good, as it was a pretty high bar, but when she'd found Nana's muffin recipe while she and Faith were going through every inch of the house, she thought she'd give it a try.

As she sipped her coffee, she flipped through the two pages of things she, Faith and Carrie had found that they needed to do at the house over the weekend. They'd searched every square inch. Jen had no idea how things had gotten so bad, but she guessed Joe was right. Wind, rain, sun and sand were tough on houses, especially wooden ones. And after years of her family objecting to repairs, it had caught up with them.

She looked up as Faith descended the steep, narrow stairs, both hands on the railing. They'd both learned from the first night that they were a good thing to use if you wanted to make it all the way down still on your feet.

Faith yawned and poured herself a cup of coffee.

"How's the list coming? Need any help?"

Jen pushed the legal pad in Faith's direction and swept her hand through her hair.

"In addition to the actual things we really need to fix, I listed out the stuff we'd need to buy for each project. The total has too many numbers in it."

Faith's eyebrows rose and she reached for her reading glasses. She whistled slowly when she took a look at the total.

"That's not very good. I mean, really not very good at all."

Jen nodded. "No kidding. And that's just fixing things that are already broken. It'd be more if we fixed things that were also ready to break."

Jen pulled on the oven mitts with seahorses embroidered on them and took the muffins out of the oven. She set them on the counter beside a stick of butter and sat back down, her chin resting on her hands.

"What are all these?" Faith waved a stack of something she'd picked up from the counter.

"What are what?" Jen replied as she reached for napkins and set them on the table.

"All these postcards. Did you get stuck in a chain mail thing again?"

Jen laughed. "No. I don't know what they are. I got the mail, but I didn't look at anything."

Faith flipped through them. "They're all from realtors, wanting to represent you with the sale of the house. Man, there are a ton."

"What?"

Jen pulled off the oven mitts and took the stack of postcards Faith held out to her. She flipped through them and groaned.

"Oh, my gosh. Look at these. These are some of the realtors who have signs everywhere down here. Look at this one—Dirk Crabtree. What a name."

Faith took a look at the postcard. "Kind of handsome, though, don't you think?"

"What? I didn't even notice. I'm just glad Greg and my dad didn't see those. That wouldn't work in our favor."

"Oh, I suppose not," Faith said as she reached for a muffin and slathered butter on it. She groaned with pleasure, her eyes closed.

"Man, your grandmother's muffin recipe is memorable. I'm going to have to walk ten times more if you're going to make these all the time."

"Uh-huh," Jen said, distracted by the stack of postcards.

"So, where do we start?" Faith asked.

Jen plopped on the sofa, giving Daisy a pat on the head when she ran in the door and rested her head on Jen's knee.

"I guess I have to call my dad or Greg. I don't have that kind of money to spare."

Faith poured another cup of coffee and handed it to Jen, then leaned against the sofa.

"Haven't you guys been sharing expenses? You and your dad and Greg?"

Jen nodded. "Yeah, but these are kind of in a different category. It's one thing to make new curtains for a bedroom or fix a leaky faucet. This list is pretty long, and I'll need everybody to agree."

Faith filled up Daisy's water bowl and got a wildly wagging tail as thanks. She patted Daisy before sitting down beside Jen.

"Well, I guess we'll just have to see what they have to say."

CHAPTER ELEVEN

"Daisy, wait!"

Jen knew Daisy was anxious to go for her evening walk, but she'd wanted to get dinner ready beforehand. She wanted to do something special since it was Friday, and she settled on barbecued chicken marinated in garlic, olive oil and rosemary with seasoned rice and barbecued zucchini. She'd sprinkled feta cheese over everything when it was done, and it was one of her favorite summer meals.

She knew Faith and Carrie were happy to help barbecue, so she pulled out the rice steamer, got the rice cooking and the chicken marinating, and was ready to go.

By that time, Daisy was extra anxious to get down to the water. Without thinking, Jen opened the gate before she'd clipped on the leash and the next thing she knew, she was chasing a speeding border collie down to the water.

Daisy had fallen in love with splashing in the waves,

and there was nothing Jen could do but try to catch up, the leash flying behind her as Faith followed close behind.

Jen, Faith and Carrie were meeting on the beach for a sunset walk and heading back up to the house afterward for a sunset happy hour on the deck and dinner.

They finally got a stroke of luck when Daisy spotted Boris, who was pulling Joe along behind him, trying to get to Daisy. When they met, Daisy finally stayed in one place long enough for Jen to clip the leash on her.

"Whew. Thanks," Jen said, flashing a grateful smile at Joe. "I don't think I ever would have caught her. She'd outlast me, for sure."

"Sure, no problem." Joe smiled at the two dogs romping in the water. "We should take them to the dog beach sometime. They could run off their leashes and we could rest and not chase them for a while."

Jen laughed and nodded. "That'd be a great idea. She could use the chance to get out some of this energy. She's killing me."

"And me too," Faith said as she caught up to them. She gulped air as she tried to catch her breath, but smiled at Joe. "Hi, Joe. Nice to see you."

Joe nodded with a little bow. "You, too, Faith. How is everything with you?"

"Great! Off for the summer—well, sort of. Teaching a couple days a week, but the rest of the time I get to stay here." She spun in a circle, her arms waving toward the beach.

"That's great. You seem as excited as Daisy."

"I think I am," Faith said, waving her arms at Carrie as she came toward them down the beach.

"Still can't miss her from a mile away, can you?" Joe asked.

Jen cocked her head at her friend's bright yellow shirt and tennis skirt with bright flowers, topped off by her orange visor. "No, you sure can't," she replied.

"Hey, you guys. Happy Friday." Carrie bent down to pet each dog with a broad smile. "It's nice to be out of the clinic. I could sure use a walk."

"Same here." Jen pulled Daisy back a bit and looked south, then north. "Which way do you guys want to go?"

"Let's go south," Carrie said. "It's high tide, and we can walk out on the pier, see if any of the surfers are any good. Andrea and her boyfriend are out there. Maybe they got lucky."

Jen hadn't seen Carrie's long-time assistant yet this year, so they got ready to head south. "Joe, you and Boris want to come along?"

"What? Uh, no. I have some work I have to do tonight. You guys have a good time."

They waved goodbye and headed south as Joe and Boris headed north.

"Work?" Carrie whispered. "I thought he was just around to help his mom."

Jen shrugged her shoulders. "He told me there were some things he had to do around the house and with the business, too. I don't know. Maybe he just didn't want to come."

"Do they still have the gondola business?" Faith asked. "I remember you said he and Allen worked there every summer through college."

"I think so." Jen couldn't remember if he'd

mentioned it that night he stopped by. It was one of the biggest businesses in the harbor, and it stood to reason that if they still owned it and his dad passed away, there'd be work to do. "We can ask him next time we see him."

They headed down the beach, Daisy leading the way.

"So what did your dad say?" Faith asked when they'd gotten into a good rhythm.

Jen sighed and shook her head. "It wasn't great. When I told him the estimate, he just didn't say a word."

"Nothing?" Carrie asked. She'd met the girls for breakfast during the week and knew what Jen was looking at.

"No. Not a word. He said he needed to talk to Greg. Asked if I wanted to call him myself, which I declined to do. Greg and I don't do well trying to work anything out anymore."

Daisy picked up a stick that was almost as big as her head. The girls laughed when she decided it needed to go with them on the walk.

Carrie walked fast but steady, her eyes glued to the high tide line. She had quite a shell collection and had specific ones she wanted to add.

"I did get him to agree to come out for the Fourth of July. Told him we'd have a barbecue, invite all the kids."

"*All* the kids?" Faith asked. "Greg and Sylvia and the kids, you mean?"

Jen sighed. "Yes, that's what I said. Anyway, he bit. Said he hadn't been down in a while and he had been wanting to visit. So we've got two weeks to fix what we can for as little as possible, spruce up the house and make it look like not so big a project. I'll call Michael and Amber and see if they can come."

"I don't know. They said they were pretty busy this summer, didn't they?" Carrie bent to pick up a shell and slipped it into the pocket of her tennis skirt.

"Yeah, but I can try. Faith, why don't you see if Maggy can come. She'd have fun, and since it's a three-day weekend, maybe she can get away." Carrie hopped over the stick that Daisy had decided she no longer wanted as she tugged at the leash, goading them all to go faster.

"Well, you needn't worry. I can come," Carrie said with a laugh. "Mom asked me to help her with a fundraiser, but that's not until Labor Day. And I still haven't decided if I'm going to do it."

Faith and Jen stopped dead in their tracks, and it took Carrie a second or two to realize she was walking alone as she was staring at the sand.

"What?"

Jen and Faith both blinked slowly in her direction. "You're actually considering saying yes?" Jen finally asked.

Carrie tipped back her visor. "Well, I don't know. She said it was just to be in charge of donations. I figured maybe you guys could help gathering things from people, local businesses. We pretty much know everybody anyway. And it's for a good cause."

"Which one? Hospital? Yacht club? Museum?" Jen asked with a wink. Carrie's mother had her hand in just about everything.

"Well, this one is *at* the yacht club, I think. Right after the Fourth of July boat parade, but *for* the children's wing of the hospital. You know I'm a sucker for kids."

"Hm," Jen said. She did know that Carrie would do whatever she could for kids.

"I'm in," Faith said. "I'll be here most of the time, so I can help on my days off."

"Well, maybe I'll say yes, then. Do something to help the kids and make some points with my mom. Goodness knows I could use some."

"Good idea. We could all use some points in our favor about now, I think."

CHAPTER TWELVE

"Who's that guy in the yard?"

Jen had had her eye on Daisy as they walked up the beach to the house and hadn't noticed the tall, blond man standing on the deck knocking on the front door. As they got closer, she noticed a clipboard in his hand and some postcards in his pocket.

"I'll go around back and open the door," Faith whispered.

Jen nodded as they all slipped in the gate. She held out her hand to the man and he smiled broadly. His eyes crinkled, and she thought he looked vaguely familiar. The slight gray around his temples was intriguing, but she wanted to keep her distance.

"Hi. Which one of you is Jen Watson?" he asked with a nod at both Jen and Carrie.

"I am."

"Oh, good to meet you. I'm Dirk, Dirk Crabtree."

At the same time Faith opened the door, Carrie burst

into a coughing fit, holding onto the post of the awning to steady herself.

"Are you all right?" Faith asked Carrie, who nodded slowly, her eyes wide.

"I'm Jen, and these are my friends Faith Donovan and—"

Carrie seemed to have suddenly caught her breath as she cut in. "Betty. Betty White. Nice to meet you."

Dirk cocked his head as he shook their hands with a quizzical look at Carrie. "Uh, Betty White. Okay, well, nice to meet you all."

Jen suddenly placed him as the realtor on one of the postcards they'd looked at before.

"So who contacted you? You're a realtor, right?"

"Why yes, yes I am." He seemed flattered that she recognized him, but Jen knew he was just doing his job. "Greg—your brother, I believe—asked if I could come and take a look at the house. Run some comps. Give him —and the family—an idea of a realistic sales price for the house."

Jen felt all eyes on her as she sat slowly on one of the deck chairs. "Oh, okay," was all she could eke out.

"Great," Dirk said, scribbling something on his clipboard. Daisy hopped up the steps after her roll on the grass and promptly shook, spraying water and sand everywhere.

Carrie held her hand over her mouth as Dirk wiped the sand and water from his very expensive pants. When he finished, he found his smile and looked from the dog to Jen.

"Shall we?" he asked.

"Um, Faith, could you—"

"Of course," Faith responded with a compassionate glance at Jen. "Right this way, Mr. Crabtree."

As the screen door swung shut, Jen dropped her head in her hands. "Greg didn't say anything about this. Nothing at all."

Carrie sat down beside Jen, wrapping an arm over her shoulder. "I'm sure he just wants to see. Just get an estimate. Prices are sky high around here. He probably just wants to know what he's dealing with."

Jen glanced in the window behind her, where Faith was giving the realtor a tour. "I know. It just—it just feels wrong. He shouldn't even be in there. Feels like we're being invaded."

Carrie stood and peeked in the window as well. "I know. I'd feel the same. But maybe it'll be bad news. Who knows? It could be in such bad shape that you can't get much for it. That'll change the game, don't you think?"

Jen looked next door at the curtain twitching. She reminded herself to take over some of Nana's muffins to Mrs. Grover. Maybe that would stop the twitching. But for now, she couldn't worry about it.

"I'll be right back," Carrie said as she went in the house, returning with a bottle of wine and glasses. She poured one for Jen and one for herself and sat back down beside her friend.

"I think they're almost done. He was in the bathroom."

Jen took a generous sip of wine and paced along the deck. She noticed that it creaked in the same place every time and made a mental note to put it on the list.

Finally, Faith and the realtor came back out. He was still scribbling on the clipboard.

He smiled and nodded at Jen. "Thanks, ladies. I think I have everything I need to give you a good quote."

"Great," Jen said with zero enthusiasm.

"Nice to meet you Faith, Miss Westland and...Miss White," he said as he closed the creaky gate behind him. "Oh, and the toilet in the main floor bathroom was running. You might want to check it out."

All three watched in silence as he got into the huge SUV that he'd parked right on the street in front of the house. How he'd gotten that parking space would remain a mystery, but realtors seemed to have special abilities when it came to things like that, Jen noted.

"Well, that was a surprise," Carrie finally said as he pulled away.

"Almost as much as a surprise as when you introduced yourself as Betty White," Faith said, sputtering through laughter. "What was that about?"

Carrie waved her hand and laughed. "I've had somebody calling the office for days asking for me and I didn't know who it was, so I didn't call back. I guess it was him. I didn't want him to know who I was."

Jen finally cracked a smile. "Okay, but Betty White? Really?"

"It was all I could think of. I've been binge-watching *Golden Girls*. It just came to me."

Faith shook her head and rolled her eyes, her silver bracelets clinking as she brushed back her hair. "I'm sure he bought it. No question."

"Hey, everything's ready for dinner. You guys hungry?"

"Absolutely." Carrie rubbed her tummy. "Just let me know how to help."

Jen watched as Dirk turned onto Newport Boulevard and made a mental note to call her brother. There was something going on, obviously, that she didn't know. And she aimed to find out what it was.

CHAPTER THIRTEEN

They'd all pitched in with dinner, each to the best of their abilities. Faith was great at getting the table set and chopping and slicing when necessary—and was great at clean-up. Carrie could barely boil water but knew her way around barbecue tongs.

"You sure do know how to barbecue," Faith said.

They plopped into comfy chairs on the top deck after everything had been cleaned up and put away.

Carrie poured a little bit more wine as they all looked out over the waves that sparkled white under the light of the moon.

"My dad insisted. Just like your dad wanted to make sure you could whistle louder than anybody, my dad wanted me to be the best barbecuer. I think maybe he wanted a son instead."

"Who says barbecue is the domain of men? When they're not around, you've got it covered for us," Faith chimed in, raising her glass in Carrie's direction. "And Jen, it was fabulous. As usual."

"Aw, glad you all enjoyed it. Faith is right. The chicken was cooked to perfection, Carrie. A little black around the edges, just how I like it."

Carrie laughed. "If I didn't know that to be true, I'd think you were lying. I did it on purpose."

They all sat in silence for a bit, listening to the crashing waves. The seagulls had gone somewhere for the night—Jen was never sure where—but they all turned as a loud rustle came from a palm tree a bit south, right over the boardwalk.

"What's that?" Carrie asked.

Faith stood and leaned closer over the railing of the balcony. "I'm not sure, but I've heard something in that palm tree every night since we've been here. Haven't seen anything, though."

It was a little difficult to see through the dark, but Jen leaned over as well.

"Whatever it is, it sure is making a ruckus. Some kind of bird, obviously."

"Obviously," Carrie said as she leaned up against the railing as well. "Maybe we can see better in the morning, see what kind of birds."

They'd been meeting early to walk Daisy, and it had been one of Jen's favorite times of the day. A couple of times, they'd run into Joe. Daisy and Boris were becoming fast friends.

Jen looked where Carrie pointed as her friend grabbed her wrist. "Oh, my gosh, look."

A tall man walked down the street wearing a black-and-white striped shirt, black pants and a red sash. He held a white straw hat in his hand.

They all watched as he approached the boardwalk. He was tall and lean, but beyond that Jen couldn't get a good look at him.

He got closer to the streetlight before they all three gasped at the same time. And before Jen could stop her, Faith whistled that cat-call whistle—not as loud as Jen could have, but loud enough for Joe to stop and turn.

He took off his hat and looked up at the balcony, and Jen would have bet that could they see better, they'd see his cheeks turning pink.

He took off his hat and gave them all a deep bow.

"Good evening, ladies."

Jen felt like she was having a moment of *deja vu*—suddenly, in front of her under the street lamp, were Allen and his best friend, Joe. Thirty years ago, and in their gondolier outfits. Just like now.

She shook her head and snapped out of it as the girls laughed and cat-called.

"Best gondolier this side of Venice," Faith shouted.

"Thank you, madam," he said with a broad smile. "The business is short-handed and I had to—well, fill in. Just like old times."

"Just like old times," Jen said quietly. A little bit louder, she said, "Would you like to come up for a drink? We're just admiring the waves."

"Oh, thank you, but no. This is a bigger workout than when I was younger. I think I need a shower. And a bed. Rain check?"

"Of course," Jen said, and they all waved as he turned the corner, the bold black and white stripes visible for quite a while down the boardwalk.

"Well, that was something," Carrie said after a bit.

"I don't think I've ever seen anything like that except in pictures. I didn't know you guys then—he looks pretty good in that get-up."

"Yes, he does," Carrie said. "He did then, and he does now."

Faith sat back down as Joe disappeared. "I knew his family owned one of the gondola companies but didn't expect he'd work there."

Jen sat down beside her. "Yes, one of the oldest and best in Newport. There are several, and they all do well, to be honest. But Joe's mom only allows them to serve authentic Italian on their tours. It's the real deal without going to Venice."

"Wow," Faith said. "It'd be fun to go on one sometime."

"They are really fun. Lots of marriage proposals, I bet, but they're a fun way to get around the harbor. See the houses. Maybe we should ask him."

Jen was quiet for a moment, remembering the times she and Joe and Allen had snuck gondolas out on top of watching fireworks. Carrie had come, too. But it seemed like a very long time ago.

"Maybe," she said quietly. She turned and looked back at the house. "Lots of memories here. All kinds. More than I've thought of in a long while."

Faith let out a deep sigh. "Doesn't seem right we might not be sitting here next summer."

Faith and Carrie nodded, and they sat quietly listening to the waves.

Jen looked back at the house again, and up and down the boardwalk. "No. It doesn't seem right at all."

CHAPTER FOURTEEN

F aith couldn't remember a time when she'd had such a fitful night's sleep with the windows open, waves lapping at the sand. She should have slept like a rock. But at least she knew why.

What Faith had thought was a good idea—to check her email—hadn't turned out to be such a good one after all.

The sound of the waves lapping at the shore lulled her into a yawn, and she realized what a long day it had been. She stood and stretched, ready to get a good night's sleep.

And then she'd had the brilliant idea to check her email. She scrolled through the faceless advertising emails she got every day and only stopped when she saw Amy's name. Her principal rarely emailed, and she'd actually been expecting a phone call before now. Faith opened it up right away and reached for her reading glasses.

. . .

Hi, Faith.

I was able to meet with Charity's principal, and it wasn't great news. Guess I was right to assume there are some "issues" here. Rather than a stellar first year, there are some problems and Charity is going to require a full-time mentor this summer. I know you and I talked about just a couple of days a week, but that's not going to work out. All the other spots are full for this summer, but I'd like to know first if you'd like to take this on. Let me know as soon as you can, please. Sorry for the change and I hope you're enjoying your time at the beach.

Amy

Faith sure hadn't seen that coming. She'd been thrilled that she could just teach two days and spend the rest with her friends at the beach. Her daughter Maggy had promised to come up from San Diego as much as she could, and she really wanted to help Jen with the repairs at the house. She'd been Jen's "helper" with design things for years, and she'd been looking forward to this for months. And now, with the possibility that the house might go on the market, Jen needed her more than ever. And she wanted to be there to help.

The last school year had been her toughest one yet, and she pinched the bridge of her nose as she got out of bed and snuggled her feet into her flip flops.

She changed from her pajamas into shorts and a soft

t-shirt, and flipped open her computer. One thing had kept her up all night as she tossed and turned, and she thought maybe she had it worked out in her head but would be more comfortable seeing it on her budget worksheet.

She punched in the numbers she'd come up with. It was pretty clear in black and white that she'd do much better if she took the assignment, but after calculating what she had been going to make only two days a week, she moved numbers around to see if she could do without for three months.

It would be tight. Very tight. She stood up and paced on the deck. The sun had peeked over the hills behind the harbor and glistened on the smooth water, boats of all sizes bobbing as the harbor met the day. The seagulls followed the fishing boats and a few sea lions squatted on the swim steps of docked boats, sunning themselves in the early morning light.

She took in a deep breath, the salty, cool air warming her. The aroma of coffee curled up the stairs, and Faith knew what she had to do. She'd planned for this, looked forward to this, and she knew someone else could help Charity as much as she could. She had something more important to do—something that mattered more to her than money.

———

Carrie stretched on the balcony and then reached for her walking shoes. She glanced at her watch—she'd need to leave soon if she was going to be at Mama's Kitchen by nine, which was what she and Faith and Jen had arranged last night. But she did have time for coffee. There was always time for coffee.

She'd fallen right into bed when she'd gotten home and when she went downstairs, she realized that her phone was beeping with missed phone messages. All from her mother.

No phone call to her mother could happen without a little coffee in her veins, so she poured herself a mug and sat on the deck, listening to the voicemails. It appeared that a decision about co-chairing the donations for the fundraiser was an emergency, by the sound of her mother's rising voice.

She supposed she'd put it off long enough, and as the caffeine began to course through her veins, she placed the call she'd been avoiding. She'd been surprised the night before when Jen and Faith had encouraged her to say yes, promising to help in any way they could. Since they wanted to help, she really had no reason to say no, and she supposed she might as well get it over with.

"Hello, Mother," she said when her mom answered.

"Oh, thank goodness. I thought you'd run off somewhere, right when I need you."

Carrie pulled the phone away from her ear and frowned at it. Run off? She rarely went anywhere and had no idea where that had come from, but she knew her mother could bring in the drama when she felt ignored. She hadn't been trying to ignore her mother, exactly. It had just taken some time for her to decide what to do.

She bit her lip and decided just to trust them. "No, I'm here. I'm calling to let you know I've decided to help.

I'll be the co-chair, but for donations only. Jen and Faith said they'd help me."

"Oh, Jen and Faith. I'd forgotten all about them."

Carrie rolled her eyes. Her mother had never forgiven Jen and Faith for—well, lots of silly things her mother perceived as bad. The list was too long to even remember, no matter how long ago.

"Well, you'll be seeing them. They want to help. And donations only. No funny business, changing it into something else."

Her mother breathed a very audible sigh. "Funny business? When have I ever—"

"Mother, you and I both know you have. There was the yacht club fundraiser where I was suddenly in charge of catering. I don't cook nor do I know about that stuff."

"Well, you're right. That was a disaster."

Jen nodded, even though her mother couldn't see her. She was right. It had definitely been a disaster.

"Right. So learn your lesson. Donations only."

Her mother sighed again. "Oh, all right. And I do appreciate it. Maude just hasn't been able to hold up her end of the bargain."

"I heard she sprained her wrist, Mom."

"There are things that are more important than pain, Carrie. You know that. You don't renege on a commitment when it comes to a fundraiser."

Carrie stifled a laugh. Her mother was dedicated to the community and had a big role to play, but if the older woman was in pain, Carrie certainly could help with letting her off the hook. It was the least she could do. Especially for such a good cause.

"Okay, whatever you say. I'll help. What do I need to do?"

"Let me find my notes." Her mother fell silent for a moment, and Carrie could almost see her reaching for a very detailed list and timeline—which would only help Carrie pull this off, so she was grateful.

"All right, here we are. You've got a co-chair. So you may as well tell Faith and Jen that they can go about their business."

A co-chair? Carrie had agreed to this assignment knowing that she, Jen and Faith would do it together. She didn't need a co-chair and certainly didn't want one.

"Mother, I don't need a co-chair. We can do this, just the three of us."

She heard her mother's familiar sniff that she made when she didn't approve.

"Well, that may be, but this gentleman is very familiar with large donors in the area and we need him to be involved."

The hair on the back of Carrie's neck bristled. "Mother, you're not trying to set me up, are you?"

Her mother's laugh was just a little too forced for her taste, but she said, "Of course not, dear. I've learned my lesson with that. He's just a nice man. I'll set up a meeting for you, too. Maybe for dinner? At the Pavilion? The foundation's treat, for all your service."

Carrie had a sneaking hunch that this wouldn't go well, but she was experienced in telling men that she wasn't interested. It really didn't matter if her mother was trying to set her up. It wouldn't work, and she might get a little help with donations after it was all said and done.

"All right. Fine. Just let me know what night and what time."

"Thank you, dear. I do appreciate it, and the foundation appreciates it as well. I'll make the reservation and let you know the details. You just go. I promise, you'll like him."

"Okay. I'll be there. What's his name? I can ask for him at the hostess station."

"He's quite the successful realtor around town. Maybe you already know him. Dirk. Dirk Crabtree."

CHAPTER FIFTEEN

J en settled Daisy beside the outdoor table she and
Faith had slid right into at Mama's Kitchen.

"Lucky day," Faith said as she looked around
at the crowded café.

"Yep. The sun is shining, there was a free table, it's
Saturday—all is right with the world."

Daisy's tongue lolled to one side and she panted after
the long walk they'd just taken on the beach. Jen slid a
bowl of water toward her that the waitress had delivered
with a smile.

Carrie rushed in, looking and sounding a little like
Daisy. She sat down and gulped a glass of water as the
waitress slid her a cup of coffee.

"Thanks, Sadie," she said gratefully. Sadie had been
waiting on them for many summers now, and it was nice
to see the familiar face.

"You're out of breath. What's up? Did you run here?"
Faith asked the question first before Jen even had a
chance to tell them.

Carrie took another gulp of water and held her hand to her chest. She seemed a little frantic. "You're not going to believe what happened."

"Spill," Jen said, leaning forward on the table. Carrie didn't frequently get flustered like this, and she couldn't wait to find out why she had. She was a little awkward, but it never seemed to bother her.

"I talked to my mom. Told her we'd be happy to take charge of the fundraiser. She was thrilled, by the way, and said to thank you both."

Jen nodded. "That's not horrible. What else?"

"Oh my gosh, she said I have a co-chair. I tried to tell her I didn't need one, but it didn't work."

Faith groaned. "I'd rather just do it ourselves."

"Me, too. But it's a done deal. Said this guy needed to be involved and knows a lot of muckety mucks. Can get bigger donations."

Jen stirred cream into her coffee. "Okay, that makes sense. So who is it?"

Carrie closed her eyes leaned back into her chair.

"Dirk Crabtree."

Both Jen and Faith stared at her for a moment, their mouths wide open, before they burst into laughter.

"You're kidding, right?"

Carrie groaned and shook her head slowly. "I wish I was. I'm not."

Faith laughed so hard she could barely catch her breath.

"So, I guess he'll find out you're not really Betty White."

Carrie gave her a quick side-eye. "Right. That'll be fun."

Jen rested her hand on Carrie's arm and tried to comfort her, even though she was still laughing. "It'll be okay."

"Well, it'll have to be. I have to meet him this week at the Pavilion for dinner."

The Pavilion was one of the oldest, most interesting restaurants in Newport, covered in lights and right on the water, with great food. Not that it mattered when you had to confess to not being Betty White.

"Will you guys go with me? You're helping with this. You're kind of like co-chairs, too."

Both Faith and Jen shook their heads in unison. "Not a chance. You don't need us, anyway. But we'll be ready for a full report afterward. You guys can make a plan, and we can execute it," Faith said.

Jen agreed. "Right. And you can see if you can get any intel about the beach house."

Carrie blinked a few times and seemed to shake it off —at least for now. "Right. Any word about the house?"

"None. I've left messages with my dad and Greg both. Nothing."

"Keep trying. And meantime, we should get on some of the repairs," Faith said.

Jen looked at Faith and wondered about the tone in her voice. She seemed a little off and the napkin she'd been holding was in shreds on her plate. "Faith, you all right?"

Jen and Carrie both sat in silence as Faith described what had happened with her summer school job.

"I want to stay and help, Jen. It means a lot to me. I want to do whatever it takes so that the house can stay in the family."

Jen's eyes misted. She knew Faith needed the money, and was touched that she'd give that up for her—for them.

"Well, then, we'd better get started. I say we do some shopping. Pick up some fabric. Spruce up the place as best we can. And maybe get on those stairs so you don't risk your life every time you go to bed."

Faith smiled softly and nodded. "I'm here to do whatever it takes."

———

Jen, Carrie and Faith spent the day walking through the shops and restaurants, asking for donations for the fundraiser if the owners weren't too busy. They'd left Daisy at home and meandered through the small streets and ended up at the Fun Zone that Jen had always thought was probably California's version of Coney Island.

It was right on the water with arcades, games, and small rides. They'd spent tons of time there as kids and with their own, and they each had a frozen banana as they sat on a bench underneath the Ferris wheel, resting their feet.

Seagulls begged for a bite, and Jen laughed as she shooed them away.

"What a beautiful day," Faith said. "I feel kind of liberated."

Jen glanced gratefully at her friend. "I bet. I'm so glad you decided to stay. We've got a lot to do."

Faith laughed. "We sure do."

"We've gotten a lot of stuff to help the effort today," Carrie said. "Want to take the ferry over to the island and check it out? There are more businesses to ask there. I haven't been in a while."

They all agreed, and in minutes they were on the ferry that went from the peninsula to Balboa Island. They sat with the cars and people who looked like tourists as it made its way across the harbor, and Jen remembered the very first time she'd been on it. Her dad had held her tightly as she stood on the bench, watching the water pass quickly beneath them. She felt the same peace every time since—and she'd been on it many times by now.

Her phone rang right about in the middle of the bay, and she would have ignored it but it was her father. "Dad, I've been calling you for days. Where have you been?"

Jen's dad paused on the other end of the line and laughed. "I've been busy."

Jen took a quick look at the phone. It wasn't like her dad to brush her off like that. She wondered once again what could have caused him to be so—busy. Especially with something as important as the status of the beach house hanging over all their heads.

She decided just to plow ahead.

"You got my estimate for the work at the beach house?"

"I did. I met Greg last night at the Mexican Kitchen and we talked it over."

Her chest tightened. Why were they talking it over without her? Again? This just wasn't right.

"Dad, I wanted to talk about it all together."

"I know, sweetheart, but it was just easier to do it over a pitcher here. Besides, we're here and you're there."

Exactly. She was staying at the beach house, fixing things every day, and they weren't. She should be in the loop.

"So, what did you talk about?"

"Well, that list you sent was pretty long. And expensive. We decided that neither of us wanted to put in that kind of money. So we contacted a realtor."

"Yeah, I met him. Dirk Crabtree. He's already been to the house."

"Oh, good," he said. "I meant to let you know. Guess I forgot. Been busy."

Jen sighed with frustration. "Has he gotten back to you yet with an estimate?"

"No, he hasn't, but I'll let you know as soon as I hear."

"Right," Jen said slowly, hoping that maybe Carrie could get some information when she met with the realtor, as her dad was less than forthcoming.

"I'm looking forward to coming to the barbecue for the Fourth. We can talk then. Nice tradition."

Jen was looking forward to the Fourth of July party, too. It was one of Nana's favorite holidays and they'd always taken the kids to the boat parade, where all of the boats were decked out in red, white and blue. And she'd planned to make all of Nana's favorites for their barbecue.

"All right. I think most of the kids are coming." In the back of her mind, she hoped that maybe a family event, one steeped in tradition and memories, might help her out of this mess. Her dad loved the beach house, too. He just needed to be reminded.

"And until then, just do the repairs that are low cost. Keep it to a minimum. I'll see you then."

She sighed as he ended the call. She filled Carrie and Faith in on what he'd said, and they looked as crestfallen as she felt.

CHAPTER SIXTEEN

They'd gone into lots of shops on the Island, most they'd been to before—and a new one that sold all kinds of unusual things. They'd spent the most time there, looking at the wares from all over the world. Faith lingered by the pillows—Jen and Faith had spent lots of time making pillows for Jen's client friends— and they were both quite enamored with the fabrics. Many had lovely beading and shiny embroidery.

"These are awesome," Faith whispered to Jen as she flashed a smile at the owner. The woman was a bit older, with long hair that was white in front and still a dark brown in a braid that hung down her back. She was very pretty and a little exotic. She introduced herself as Patti, explained that she traveled the world to fill her shop and thanked them for coming.

Outside, Carrie plopped down on a bench and rubbed her calves. "I think I need to call it quits for the day. At least the walking part. My feet are tired."

Faith and Carrie agreed, and they crossed back over

on the ferry and headed home. As they walked toward the beach house, Jen looked up and pointed out all the "For Sale" signs along the way. In between the houses with signs, the streets were dotted with new construction projects.

"Wow, I haven't been down this far on the peninsula for a while. So many of these houses have been torn down. These new ones look so modern," Carrie said.

Jen agreed. "Yeah. There aren't too many of the old original ones left."

"Big change," Faith agreed. "How crazy is that? I wonder what these people have to pay, just to have the house torn down and build another."

"Let's get home and look on Zillow. We can find out what these places sold for. Might give us some kind of idea what the house is worth, and what we're up against." Jen couldn't believe that she hadn't thought to look earlier.

"Great idea," Carrie said.

They picked up the pace and reached the house in just a few minutes. Faith opened the gate—wincing as it creaked—and laughed at Daisy's nose plastered on the window.

When the puppy saw them coming up the steps, she pushed away from the window and they all three jumped toward the door as a loud crash rang out.

"Thank goodness we got the doorknob replaced," Faith said as they rushed through the front door.

Jen surveyed the damage as quickly as she could. One of the lamps in the corner was a casualty, and it looked like some of the walnut paneling had been knocked from the wall during the event.

Pillow fluff was everywhere, and the pillow that had given its life for Daisy's entertainment rested at the foot of the stairs.

"Oh, goodness," Carrie said slowly. "Looks like she would have rather come with us."

"No doubt." Faith reached for a trash bag and began to pick up the pillow stuffing. Carrie straightened the lamp—or tried to. It was never going to recover.

Jen tried to stick the paneling back on the wall before she realized it would have to be a major project. And as she got a good look at the wall behind the paneling, it was evident that taking the paneling off would unleash a whole slew of things to be done with the drywall behind it.

"The toilet's still running," Carrie hollered from the bathroom.

Jen sat down hard at the kitchen island, the orange plastic stool creaking as she did. The tears she'd struggled to keep at bay prickled. She looked around the room and shook her head.

"I don't know how to make this work," she said softly, resting her elbows on the counter and dropping her chin in her hands.

Carrie handed her a tissue. "There has to be something we can do."

"Right," Faith said as she rested her hand on Jen's shoulder. "We'll think of something. We always do."

Jen was all out of ideas. With her father and brother

not cooperating and not even interested in fixing up the place, what could she do alone?

Faith snapped her fingers.

"Didn't the contractor say that the little apartment over the garage was in the best shape of anything? Since it was newer?"

Jen nodded. "Yes, he did. At least that's one thing we've got going for us."

"What if you get renters or something? We could put an ad on Craigslist. The income would cover expenses and maybe a little more, even, for repairs."

Carrie and Jen exchanged quick glances.

"That's not a bad idea, Jen. Lots of people rent out rooms or small apartments to help cover costs. And there are lots of people looking. The university isn't that far. Lots of the students live around here."

Jen's mood brightened a bit. "That's something to look at, for sure."

Daisy scratched at the door and looked back at Jen.

"Oh, gosh, I completely forgot she needs to go out. We're lucky we didn't have any messes to step in." She reached for the door after giving Daisy a grateful pat.

"I'll take her for a quick walk. You guys get out the laptop and see what you can find on Craigslist for rents. And then we can check Zillow."

Jen's mind was on the dilemma at hand, and she opened the gate as she reached for the leash. Daisy nosed the gate open before Jen could get the leash on her and was off like a shot, headed straight for the beach.

"Oh, great," Jen said as she took off behind Daisy.

CHAPTER SEVENTEEN

"Daisy! Daisy!" Jen shouted as she ran toward the boardwalk. She could almost hear Mrs. Grover *tsk-tsk* as the curtain twitched when she ran by.

She hopped over the big splat of something yucky under the palm tree and wondered again what it was that was making such a big commotion up there. She followed Daisy straight to the beach, leash in hand to grab her, hoping Daisy would stop before she plowed right into the water.

She didn't. The puppy didn't let up even a bit as she headed straight for the waves. Jen didn't exactly want to follow her in for a swim and looked quickly up and down the beach to see how many people were looking at her disapprovingly for having her dog off a leash. They'd understand if they knew how fast Daisy was.

She waited for a moment, calling Daisy every once in a while, hoping that her energy would dissipate a little faster. Finally, Daisy stopped jumping, shook with a big cloud of water droplets and began to walk in Jen's direction.

"Good girl. Come on, just a little further," Jen said, firmly gripping the clip of the leash, ready to get Daisy secure and back home.

She and Daisy both turned toward a loud bark up the boardwalk.

"No, Boris, not now," Jen exclaimed when Daisy's tail began to wag furiously, and the puppy took off like a shot toward her friend.

"Ugh," Jen said before she took a deep breath and ran behind Daisy toward Joe's house.

Daisy arrived on Joe's porch way before Jen did, and she was out of breath when she got there. She bent over, resting her hands on her knees for a moment while Daisy and Boris rolled around on the porch.

When she looked up, Joe was smiling down at her, with the collar of a dog in each hand. He winced for a moment as Daisy shook, sand and water flying everywhere, but his smile never faded.

"Did you lose something?" he asked as Jen hooked the leash to Daisy's collar.

"Whew. Yes. Thanks."

"No problem." Joe closed the gate behind Jen and gestured to a rocking chair on the porch. "Need a rest?"

Jen laughed as she fell into the rocking chair. She let Daisy play with Boris in the courtyard, but left the leash attached just in case.

"Yes, thanks. That was quite a workout."

"She got away from you, eh? It happens," he said, smiling at the dogs as they played.

Jen agreed. "She's been great, really. First time this has happened."

"Well, it was bound to happen sometime. Glad she had a familiar place to run to, honestly."

Jen couldn't have agreed more, and glanced around at the familiar porch. They'd all spent many hours here back in the day—she, Allen and Joe, with the eventual addition of Claudia. It felt like a familiar old set of slippers, and she leaned back into the chair while she caught her breath.

She looked up as the screen door creaked, and Joe's mom peeked her head out.

"Jen, is that you?"

Jen stood and smiled, gratefully accepting the older woman's warm hug. That felt good, too.

"Mrs. Russo, it's so nice to see you."

"And you, dear. It's been a long time. A very long time."

Joe had stood also and smiled at the two women. "Way too long."

"Thank you for the sauce, Mrs. Russo. We made ravioli to go with it, and it was fantastic. Just like it's always been."

Mrs. Russo gasped in shock. "Frozen ravioli?"

Jen took a quick glance at Joe, and he shrugged as he stood behind his mother, his smile wide.

"Oh, yes, I'm sorry. I don't know how to make ravioli from scratch. It was the best we could do."

Mrs. Russo shook her head. "That won't do. Why don't you girls come for dinner next weekend? I'll show you how to make ravioli. The right way. The only way."

"Uh, that would be wonderful," Jen stammered, her eyebrows raised. "I've always wanted to learn how."

"Good. See you then, and bring an appetite."

She waved at Jen and went back into the house. Joe peeked in the house until his mother was nowhere in sight.

"I don't remember her ever offering to teach someone how to make her ravioli. Well, once she offered to teach Claudia but Claudia declined. I don't think my mother has ever offered again, as far as I know."

Jen whistled quietly. "Wow, I'm honored. Faith and Carrie won't know what's going on, but they're good helpers. I can't wait."

Joe nodded. "It'll be fun. And I'll make sure I don't have to fill in at work that night. The gondolier outfit might be a little bit much, and I wouldn't want to miss anything."

Jen laughed and reached for Daisy's leash. "Great. I'd better get back. I'll see you guys next weekend, and thanks for corralling Daisy for me."

She headed out the gate but turned to look back and wave at Joe and Boris on her way down the boardwalk.

———

By the time Jen got back to the house, Faith and Carrie had spent time on Zillow and Craigslist and had good information—and the sun was beginning to set.

"What took you so long? Must have taken Daisy a long time to run out of steam." Faith handed Jen a glass of wine, and they all sat on the porch.

Faith had a legal pad on her lap, and Carrie had the laptop. Jen shared the dinner invitation and they both were excited.

"Oh, wait. I can't go. That's the night I have to meet with what's-his-face," Carrie said with a frown.

Faith frowned as well. "Maybe we could change the night?"

Jen shook her head. "No, I don't think that would be a good idea. She never offers to share her recipes. I don't want to rock the boat."

"That's okay," Carrie said. "It would be wasted on me, anyway, and Faith is a better prep assistant. I'll take my lumps as Betty White and see what I can find out about the housing market."

"Great. That'll work." Jen pointed at the notepad on Faith's lap. "What did you guys find out?"

Faith leaned forward and bounced a little with excitement. "Well, there are lots of rentals listed on Craigslist, and if we put in an ad, I bet you'd get a lot of bites. It's not a bad amount at all for rent. It could go a long way toward paying taxes and there'd be extra for repairs."

Jen's heart lightened at the prospect. Maybe there was hope, after all, if she could convince her dad and brother just to let things be.

"That's the good news," Faith added, a little bit more quietly.

Jen leaned back in her chair and closed her eyes. "Uh-oh."

Carrie reached for the wine bottle and topped off Jen's glass. She nodded when Jen asked, "Am I going to need that?"

Faith handed over the notepad, and Jen's eyes flew open. She almost couldn't catch her breath at the number —there were so many zeroes.

"You can't be serious." She looked back at the house and up at the hold in the awning. "Even like this? The stairs? The toilets? Everything?"

Faith nodded slowly and pointed at the beach view. "It seems like that's the big seller. I could be wrong—I'm not a professional. But you know there aren't all that many of these houses left. The newly built ones are a lot more than that, if you can imagine. And very few right on the beach with a view of the harbor, also. It's unique."

"Wow." Jen tossed the notepad on the glass coffee table. "If Greg gets a whiff of that, I bet it's all over."

Carrie groaned. "Sylvia's family's got money. Why would he care?"

"His faith and loyalty remain to be seen, I'm afraid. I don't hold out much hope. I've called at least ten times to remind him about the party on the Fourth, and he hasn't even bothered to call back."

"He has to come," Carrie said. "All the kids are coming, aren't they? I mean, except Max all the way from Boston. And your dad. It'll be the perfect time to try to make your case."

Jen stood and leaned against the railing as the waves crashed on the shore. She closed her eyes as the warm breeze warmed her face. She couldn't imagine not standing here, feeling this.

"Yep. We'll just have to keep trying, and make the best case we can."

Carrie and Faith both nodded, and Jen knew that they'd all give it their best try. And if that didn't work, at least they had each other.

CHAPTER EIGHTEEN

J en couldn't believe her good luck. She stood in Mrs. Russo's kitchen, mesmerized by the smell of the sauce that filled the kitchen.

"Mrs. Russo, I can't believe you made sauce, too. I didn't expect that. I know it takes hours and hours."

"It does," Joe said. "She insisted."

Mrs. Russo patted her gray hair that she'd pulled into a bun and slipped an apron over her dress. Although the apron was clean, it had obviously been worn for many years, the pockets a little frayed at the top. Jen thought she might even remember it from years and years ago.

She handed Jen and Faith aprons and turned to her son. "Joey, put yours on."

Joe rolled his eyes and smiled at Jen as he reached into the pantry and took out a white apron with a red heart patched onto the chest. Jen smiled back at him and tried to stifle a laugh.

"Aw, that's so sweet," Faith said as she put on her apron. "Looks like you've had that for a while."

Joe nodded slowly.

"I gave it to him when he was a little boy. Got an extra big one for him to grow into. If he was going to learn to cook, it needed to be the right way."

"Yep, and I've worn it ever since, Ma."

"He's a good boy," she whispered to Jen and Faith. "But don't tell him. It'll go to his head."

Joe pretended he hadn't heard her, but Jen was certain he had as they were all crowded in the very small kitchen.

Mrs. Russo showed Jen how to roll the pasta that she'd made earlier, handing her a note card with the recipe on it. "I know you like to cook, so all I want to show you with the pasta dough is the consistency you're aiming for. A little here, a little there, but this is what it's supposed to feel like." She handed Faith and Jen each a ball of dough that they squished in their hands.

"Joey's making the filling over there. Two different kinds. A basic sausage and one with wild mushrooms."

Jen leaned over Joe's shoulder and took in a deep breath. It smelled heavenly—garlic, onions, maybe even a little marsala wine. She smiled up at Joe as he stirred. He smiled down at her and handed her a spoon.

"Here you go. Make yourself useful, as Ma says."

Mrs. Russo nodded. "That's right. Come over here, Faith. We'll roll out some of this dough while the fillings are cooking. I need to use the dining room table, as there's not enough room in here for the big sheets."

Faith shrugged her shoulders and smiled at Jen. She followed Mrs. Russo through the swinging kitchen door into the dining room.

Jen laughed and said, "Faith's not a big cook, but she's a good sport."

"I remember that about her," Joe said as he picked up his sauté pan and swished the contents around in a circle.

Jen did the same with hers and was grateful that nothing sloshed out the sides.

"This is so fun. Thanks for inviting us."

Joe nodded. "It's nice to be all be back together. We had so much fun. I've missed it."

"You're enjoying being here? You don't miss your old life?"

Joe paused for a moment and looked around the kitchen. "You know, I thought it might be hard. My life in Chicago was much different. We lived in the city, in a high-rise apartment. When Claudia and I split up—which had been coming for years and was the right thing to do —I thought I'd just continue. Walked to work at the accounting firm, everything was close by. When dad passed and I came home, I didn't really know what to expect."

"And?" Jen prodded, wondering what it would be like to be away for a long time and come back home. She'd always been home.

"Ma and I have had lots of time together. It's been nice. Learning a lot about my dad. Missing him. Going through his things. Seeing you guys. It's been nice. Nicer than I thought."

"Good," Jen said. "And gondoliering has to be keeping you in shape, too." She couldn't help but laugh and was relieved that he laughed, too.

"Good grief, that get-up. But yeah, until we make a

decision about the business, I am filling in when anybody needs help, keeping the books and doing whatever has to happen."

"Taking the occasional gondolier shift, too, clearly."

"Clearly, yes. But you're right. It's good exercise. And people are so excited to go, it's kind of nice. Seeing my hometown through other people's eyes. And I can share stuff about Newport that they don't know. And they appreciate it."

"That's fantastic. And I, for one, am very glad that you're here. It's been nice catching up."

Joe nodded and poured the contents of each saucepan into a separate dish. He collected big spoons, a roller and something that looked to Jen like a pizza cutter.

"Grab those bowls. These should be cool enough in a minute. Ma will be ready to fill by now and she doesn't like to wait."

"Okay, right behind you. Obviously, you've done this once or twice before."

Joe laughed and rolled his eyes. "More times than I can count." He pushed his hip against the swinging door and held it open for Jen to go through.

Jen followed along closely as Mrs. Russo showed her how to roll the dough and make the ravioli. As they worked, they talked about Newport and how much it had changed over the years, and Jen shared a bit about the dilemma with the house. Mrs. Russo had given her a very sympathetic look and nodded her head.

As the ravioli boiled, Jen and Faith cleared off the dining room table and set it with Joe's direction. In no time, they were eating a delicious, authentic Italian meal.

"Mrs. Russo, this is just fantastic. I'm stuffed," Faith said as she set down her fork and leaned back in her chair.

"Eat some more, all of you."

Jen, Faith and Joe laughed, but Joe took one more bite to satisfy his mother.

"Delicious, Mrs. Russo. Thank you so much for sharing how to make it. Now, if I can get your sauce recipe out of you, my life will be complete."

Joe and his mother exchanged smiles.

"Not likely," Joe said. "It's a family gravy recipe, and I don't think she's ever shared it. Not even with me."

Jen's ears perked up when he used the word gravy. She knew several older Italian women and they all referred to their sauces as gravy.

Mrs. Russo nodded. "Not until it's time. If I tell you all how to make it, you won't need me anymore. I'll tell you what. Next we can make my family's cheesecake. Best Italian cheesecake ever. More like ricotta pie but better than New York style. You'll see."

"I'd be honored," Jen said, and Joe winked at her.

Over dinner, Jen and Faith had talked about the fundraiser they were helping Carrie with. Mrs. Russo had clearly been thinking about it.

"Jen, you know Joey and I have been going through some of my dear departed husband's things. He had quite a collection of memorabilia, and I don't want it all. Neither does Joey. How about if you guys go through it and see what you think might be good for the auction?"

Joe paused for a moment and looked at his mother.

"You sure? Last we spoke you didn't know what you wanted to keep."

"You know, I've already taken the few things I do want. The things that remind me most of your father. You can take anything that's in that room of his—if you can get in it." She turned to Jen and patted her hand. "It might be all junk, Jen, but you're welcome to anything at all."

"Thank you, Mrs. Russo. We'll do that. And maybe it'll be helpful for us to clean it out."

"You're welcome, dear. And it's not just an excuse to get you to come back. I promise." Jen smiled as Mrs. Russo winked at Joe on her way to the kitchen to get the coffee.

They chatted for a bit longer, and as Joe cleared the coffee cups, Jen noticed an almost-finished crossword puzzle on the sideboard. She picked it up and read the clue for the one remaining word.

"I love crossword puzzles," she said as she smiled at Mrs. Russo. "Want some help with this one?"

Mrs. Russo tapped her cheek with her finger. "Joey and I have been staring at that one for days now. Neither of us can get it. If you can, please, be my guest. It'd be great to finish that puzzle. 'Strips in a club.' We just can't get it."

Jen squinted at the clue and looked at the surrounding letters. After a moment she laughed and looked up at Joe.

"You guys are going to hate me when I tell you."

She handed the folded newspaper to Mrs. Russo and the pencil to Joe. She took great pleasure at the flabbergasted looks on their faces when she told them the answer. "Bacon."

Joe's mouth hung open, and then he laughed loud and long as his mother filled in the letters.

"Well, look at that, Joey. She did it."

He rested his hand on his mother's shoulder with an appreciative glance at Jen. "Thanks for that. Another one down."

"Any time," Jen said. She glanced at Faith, who was enjoying the entire scene as much as she was from the look on her face. She almost hated to leave.

CHAPTER NINETEEN

Carrie could hardly believe that an entire week had gone by and that the night she'd been dreading—her meeting with Dirk—had arrived.

She'd considered asking the girls their opinions about what to wear, but she realized she didn't really care. It wasn't like it was a date, and the prospect of having to explain to Dirk that she wasn't really Betty White—obviously—didn't sound like much fun.

But she'd had her reasons. The guy had been bugging Andrea at the clinic, and he should have gotten the hint. She'd have called him back if she'd wanted to, and he'd never stated his reason for calling anyway. She squared her shoulders, ready to defend her ruse. She pulled on a pair of jeans and a cream-colored light sweater. And that was as dressed up as she was willing to get.

She did slip on her favorite flip-flops that had tiny seashells on them, but just because they were comfortable.

He was going to get what he got, and he was lucky she was willing to co-chair with him anyway.

It was a lovely, warm night, and she decided to walk to the Pavilion. It wasn't very far, and she could stop by Jen's on the way back and tell the girls what she'd found out since it was on the way.

"Well, you look nice."

Carrie stopped and looked up at Jen's porch. She hadn't even realized that she was passing by until Jen caught her attention. She looked down at her jeans and sweater.

"I do? That wasn't what I was going for."

"I might have suggested something a little nicer, but you look very pretty. Makes your hair look blonder."

"Thanks, I think," Carrie said as she nodded at Faith as she stepped onto the porch.

"Very nice," Faith said, and this time Carrie could feel the heat in her cheeks.

"This is not a date. It's work. I'm on recon for the beach house and trying to involve myself as little as possible in the fundraiser. It's work," she protested, but she could hear them chuckling as she continued down the boardwalk.

She shook it off and headed toward the Pavilion. When she arrived, the hostess smiled at her, but Carrie noticed her smile was a little pinched.

"Hello, Dr. Carrie," the young girl said. Carrie looked at her teeth—she couldn't help it—and noticed that the girl's braces had fixed things quite nicely.

"Hello, Jessica. Your teeth look lovely."

The hostess glanced in both directions, almost in a panic. She loved being a dentist—unfortunately, very few of her clients were ever happy to see her. Or wanted to come to the clinic. Hazard of the profession, she supposed, but it wouldn't be awful if somebody ever said thanks.

"Are you here alone?" Jessica said as she reached for a menu, her surprise at seeing her dentist seeming to have worn off.

"No. I'm meeting somebody. Dirk. Dirk Crabtree."

Jessica smiled wide. "Oh, of course. Mr. Crabtree. He's here already. He's talking to some people, but I'll take you over."

Carrie followed the hostess through the restaurant, bracing herself for her confession. She hoped he had a good sense of humor. He'd seemed like he might, and she hoped her luck held out.

She stopped dead in her tracks when she spotted him. And the people he was talking to. Friends of her parents. From the yacht club.

"Mr. Crabtree, your dinner guest has arrived."

Dirk stood and turned to Carrie, his eyes registering his surprised and a touch of laughter.

"Ms. White? How nice to see you again, but I'm scheduled to meet with Carrie. Carrie Westland."

"Hello, Carrie. Nice to see you again," Dr. Mendoza said, with a smile and a nod. His wife nodded as well before they headed over to their own table.

She did her best not to roll her eyes and took the seat next to him. He sat down and leaned forward, his elbows on the table.

"Well, I can tell this is going to be quite a story," he said, his eyes twinkling. "And I can't wait to hear it."

"Same here," Carrie mumbled under her breath.

The waitress came for their drink order, and Carrie ordered a glass of merlot to his Manhattan. He rested his elbow on the back of his chair as he leaned back and smiled at her.

"Well?"

Carrie took a deep breath and spilled her story. He laughed several times as she explained that she'd been caught off guard, hadn't wanted to talk to him, and just blurted out "Betty White" as she'd been watching *The Golden Girls*.

He listened intently as he sipped his Manhattan and even though she tried not to look at him, she couldn't help but notice he was handsome. And because he wasn't outright laughing at her—and wasn't angry either—she decided maybe it wouldn't be so bad to work with him.

"I don't think I've ever had anyone go to such great lengths to avoid me before. Or if they did, they were better at it than you are."

"Fair enough," she said with a laugh, glad that the story was out and over with.

"I was only calling to see if you might be interested in selling the property that the clinic is on. It's part of my job, to find properties that might be desirable for my clients. No offense intended."

"Again, fair enough. I don't want to sell, though. I love my job, and I've worked very hard building my practice. In fact, the hostess is one of my patients."

Dirk leaned back in his chair and looked over at the

hostess, who was sharing her bright, white smile with everyone in the lobby.

"Nice job there. I can see why Newport would need you to stay in practice. I won't bother you with that question again."

Carrie smiled and nodded as she took a sip of her merlot. Maybe this wouldn't be so bad after all, and they could just get right to the business of the fundraiser. She certainly hoped so.

By the time Dirk's Chilean sea bass and Carrie's filet mignon were gone, they'd come up with a plan. Dirk was efficient, and Carrie was grateful because she'd never done this before.

"So if we do all the wrapping beforehand, get all the auction sheets set up and ready to be put out, we should be in great shape."

Carrie nodded vigorously when the waiter suggested creme brûlée for dessert, as it was one of her favorites—especially at the pavilion. Dirk ordered a cappuccino but didn't say no when Carrie offered him a spoon to share the rich, creamy dessert.

In the most nonchalant voice Carrie could muster, she finally asked the question she'd been holding all night.

"So, any news about Jen's house?" She looked down at the creme brûlée and tried to feign disinterest, as if she were just making conversation.

"I shouldn't really be talking about it with you, as you're not the client, but generally speaking, I'm pretty pleased with what I've found. The location is spectacular, and at the right price I think we could have an offer pretty quickly."

Carrie's pretense of indifference disappeared, along with the last bite of custard.

"Oh," she said. "That's too bad."

Dirk's eyebrows rose as he took a sip of his coffee. "Too bad? I thought—well, I know her father and brother, whom I've spoken with also, are quite eager to sell."

"That's them, not Jen," she said slowly, dabbing at the corners of her mouth with her linen napkin. "In Jen's view, nothing could be worse."

Dirk leaned back in his chair, frowning. "I don't understand."

Carrie took a deep breath and explained the situation to Dirk. She told him about how they'd all grown up there, learned to swim there, what had happened to Allen and how Jen looked forward to raising grandkids there.

When she finished, he whistled and leaned back in his chair. He rubbed the back of his neck and turned to look at the view of the harbor.

"I guess I can understand that. No matter how high the price is, with a third of the profits, she'd never get another house down here."

"No," Carrie said. "And she knows it. We all know it."

Dirk paid the check and stood, scooting Carrie's chair out for her and holding out his arm for her.

She slipped her arm through his and looked up at him. "It's just a pretty sad state of affairs," she said as they left the restaurant.

"Can I offer you a ride home?" Dirk asked when they reached his SUV.

Carrie shook her head. "Thanks, but I think I could

use a breath of fresh air. And I appreciate your help with the fundraiser. I imagine I'd make quite a mess of it on my own."

He smiled and nodded, tipping an invisible hat in her direction as he turned and left.

She started her walk toward Jen's house, wondering if there was anything at all to be done about this situation. She was afraid that there wasn't.

CHAPTER TWENTY

Jen and Faith had been back at the beach house for only a couple of minutes, but long enough for Faith to get the binoculars. They took turns peering at the palm tree, trying to figure out what could possibly be making so much noise—and such a big mess.

They'd been working on the house constantly for the past week and hadn't been outside as much as they'd hoped they would be—they hadn't even gone paddleboarding yet. But every night as they watched the sunset, the racket from that palm tree almost drowned out their conversation.

"I think it's probably birds."

Jen laughed as Faith handed her the binoculars.

"I'm sure it's birds. What else would it be up in a palm tree?"

"We've both had rats in the palm trees before. Could have been a rat, but I think whatever it is is too big. They seem to be more active in the early morning. Maybe I'll sleep on the deck and see if I can get a better look in the morning."

"Ah, you guys are still up." Carrie climbed onto the porch and sat down.

Jen set the binoculars down and stepped over Daisy, getting back to her chair.

"Yep, we are. We had a really nice time. The ravioli was out of this world. How did you fare?"

Carrie drummed her fingers on the arm of the chair. "Believe it or not, after we got over all the ridiculousness that was Betty White, it was kind of fun. He's all right. Could be worse."

"Whew," Faith said. "We were a little worried about you, to be honest."

"Worried? Why? Because my own mouth is my worst enemy?" Carrie laughed.

"Something like that," Jen said. "So, what's the deal with the fundraiser?"

"Well, he seems to be pretty organized. Good pick by my mom, actually. He's going to take care of the bigger items, and he was fine with us getting smaller ones. You know, restaurant gift certificates, stuff like that. He's going to hit up the bigger companies for things with a higher dollar value. Maybe a week at a timeshare in Hawaii. Stuff like that."

The palm tree rustled again, and Jen reached for the binoculars.

"That sounds great. Should make a lot of money for the hospital. Oh, Joe's mom said we could take our pick from his dad's belongings. The ones in that room he was always in."

Carrie sat up, her eyes wide. "You're serious?"

Jen frowned, not sure why Carrie was so interested.

"Sure. She said so. Joe said he'd go through it with me another time. Why?"

Carrie stood and began to pace the deck. "Don't you remember the time we snuck in that room? He guarded it like Fort Knox. Never let anyone in."

Faith gestured for the binoculars and Jen handed them over.

"Vaguely. Hm, now that you mention it, wasn't it a lot of Disney stuff?"

"Yes, exactly. And model trains. He really was quite a collector."

"Well, that's good. She really didn't want any of it. But if it's stuff that's worth a lot of money, we should let her know that before we take it, don't you think?"

Carrie sat and tapped her chin. "Sure. I think maybe my mom has someone who could help us with that. Or maybe Dirk."

"Oh, Dirk. Mm-hm. We'll ask Dirk," Faith said with a sly smile.

"Stop. He's nice. That is all."

"Fair enough," Jen said. "Any info about the beach house?"

Carrie snapped her fingers. "Oh, I almost forgot. He said that he's almost ready to make a recommendation about a price. He's going to call your dad this week. Perfect timing for you all to talk about it next weekend at the barbecue."

Jen didn't hold out much hope that it would change anything. They hadn't had any luck at all interviewing potential renters, so that wasn't the answer. Either the people were older and didn't want to navigate the stairs, or younger and couldn't afford it. So she had no Plan B to present her family with. She'd just have to rely on the memories and hope she could tug at their heartstrings. But she was pretty positive that wasn't going to be enough.

CHAPTER TWENTY-ONE

J en tingled with excitement the morning of the Fourth of July. She and Faith had spent all week planning, in between house projects. They'd patched the paneling, secured the stairs, stopped the toilet from running, and fixed the creaky gate. Jen felt sure that when her family came, at least nothing would fall apart—at least not until after they'd left.

But it was all cosmetic, and she knew it. They'd patched the awning, but they still needed a new one. The roof wasn't going to last too many more winters, and half of the windows wouldn't even open. With any luck, nobody would even try.

Her son Michael and his wife were both coming, and Faith had gotten a "maybe" from Maggy. Jen knew her dad would be there, and Greg had finally relented and responded to her numerous texts with a "Sure." She had no idea who was coming with him—hopefully his wife, at minimum—but she made enough of Nana's famous potato salad just in case.

They'd timed lunch with the Fourth of July Old Glory Boat Parade that American Legion sponsored every year. In some years past, they'd decorated a boat and ridden in it themselves, but this year, Jen wanted to make sure they had plenty of time to talk about the house. She needed to know what was going to happen so that she could plan what she was going to do.

Faith busied herself with party preparations—they were barbecuing ribs and adding baked beans and corn on the cob and had made oodles of potato salad. Everything was almost ready. There wasn't much left to do, since they'd made apple pies the day before.

Jen and Faith both stopped dead in their tracks as a huge blue heron with a fish in its mouth walked up from the beach, took flight and made a beeline for the palm tree they'd been spying on. The tree burst into a ball of noise and activity.

"Sounds like World War III in there," Faith said, reaching for the binoculars. "Guess they don't like each other too much."

"That's weird." Jen took the binoculars that Faith held out and took a look. "Faith, wait a minute. I think those are babies."

"What?" Faith took the binoculars and looked through them again. "Oh, wow, I think you're right. They look pretty young, but they're still kind of big."

"How exciting. We can watch them grow up. Or kill each other, if that's what they're doing."

"Ugh, I don't want to see that," Faith said, setting the binoculars down and turning back to the task at hand.

"Herons?" Carrie looked up into the palm tree as she passed under it, carefully stepping over a big pile of —something.

"We think so. Would that be a possibility?" Faith asked.

Carrie nodded as she came through the gate, carrying a jar of pickles. She held it out to Jen with a sheepish grin. "It was all I could think of."

"Thanks," Jen said, surprised that Carrie remembered to bring anything at all, but grateful that she had.

Carrie turned back to Faith. "Yes, sure could be. They're all over at the top of the peninsula. And by some of the car dealerships. They're having a terrible time with them dropping those big piles of—debris—onto some of the new cars. Really expensive ones. And they can't move the birds or take out the trees. California, you know. They're not real happy."

"Who knew?" Faith asked, taking one last peek through the binoculars. "They are sure beautiful birds."

"Yeah, but lousy housekeepers. Or maybe good ones, I guess, as all that stuff isn't inside their nests anymore."

"That's one way to look at it," Jen said, setting the last bowl on the table and glancing at her watch. "They should all be here any minute."

As if on cue, Jen's son Michael and his wife Amber appeared.

"Grandpa's right behind us," Michael said to Jen before he turned to Faith and Carrie. "And how are my bonus moms? Haven't seen you guys in a long time."

Carrie and Faith both laughed and squeezed them all

with hugs, one at a time. They'd barely had time to say hello before Jen's dad walked in the gate with a woman she'd never seen before on his arm. Jen froze in place at the sight, and everybody behind her fell into silence at the same time.

"Hello, Dad," Jen finally squeaked out, giving him a peck on the cheek as the woman he'd brought with him took a step forward. Jen turned toward her, her hand outstretched. "I don't believe we've met. I'm Jim's daughter, Jen."

The woman nodded. "I've heard so much about you. I'm Susanna. I've been looking forward to meeting you for such a long time."

"A long time?" Jen echoed, glancing at her father. He just shrugged and walked up the steps, hugging his grandchildren, then Faith and Carrie. Suddenly, Jen realized that all eyes were on her and Susanna, a bit of anxiety trickling through the group as they watched in silence.

"Yes, a long time. Your father and I have been dating for several months now."

"Several months?" Jen echoed again, turning back to see her dad shrug one more time and turn to go in the house.

"Yes, and we've been having so much fun. It's so nice to finally see the beach house. Jim talks about it a lot. It's lovely."

Jen sighed and gave in on this recent development. Her mom had been gone for a very long time—it wasn't that. She wanted her dad to be happy. But why hadn't he told her? Why were there suddenly so many secrets in her family? She just wanted it to stop and get everything out in the open, so she turned and smiled at Susanna, held out her arm, and welcomed her into the house.

————

While everybody chatted and ate, Jen bounced between checking her phone for a message from her brother and looking down the street, hoping he'd walk up. She gave up by the time all that was left of the ribs were a bowl full of bones and the corn was down to nubs.

Her dad and Michael hooted and hollered at the boats as they passed, cheering louder for the ones with the better decorations. Jen took the last of the empty plates into the kitchen, where Faith, Carrie and Jen's daughter-in-law, Amber, washed dishes.

"No Greg?" Faith asked as she handed Amber a platter to dry. There was no dishwasher in the house, so they all were experienced with chipping in to do dishes.

Jen took another quick glance out the window and down the street.

"Nope. He said he was going to come. I just don't understand him anymore."

Amber handed the platter to Carrie, who put it back in the cupboard over the refrigerator that had been its home for the past decades.

Faith sat at the kitchen island, hopping up as the orange counter stool creaked.

"Oh, goodness. Seems like things are getting old around here."

Jen sighed. "I know. But nobody wants to pitch in the money to get new stuff."

"I heard a little bit about that from Michael." Amber stood and walked around the living room.

Pictures of her wedding to Michael held their place among pictures of Michael as a baby—all the kids as babies. More recent pictures of them when they had learned to swim, and even more recently when they were teenagers with surfboards.

"Is this you?" Amber asked, pointing at a picture with two young teenage girls in bikinis and surfboards of their own. "You and Carrie?"

Carrie crossed over and peered at the picture Amber was pointing to.

"Oh, wow. Yeah. It is. Right before your mother-in-law swore she'd never surf again. Kind of got rolled by the waves."

Jen laughed. "Hey, I did my best to fit in as a California girl. My hair turned green from swimming, so there's that. But I never got the hang of surfing. Didn't like the sand up my nose, I guess."

"No, but you hung in there sailing with the boys. That was never my thing. Not after they beat us in that sabot race one summer."

Jen reached for a photo on the mantle and handed it to Amber.

"This is Michael's dad and me that day. They beat us, but when Carrie turned to other sports, Allen and Joe kind of decided to let me tag along. I learned a lot."

"Yeah, and she taught me," Faith said. "I bet we could give them a run for their money now."

Amber ran her hand over the glass on the picture.

"I'm so sorry I never met Michael's dad. And his friend Joe. I've heard a lot about them."

Jen nodded and put the picture back in its place on the mantle.

"Just so happens he's turned up this summer. Maybe you'll get a chance to meet him." She turned to look around the room—at all the pictures and memories. "A lot has happened in this place."

"I know, and there's more to come," Amber said as she walked the room and looked at all the pictures on the wall.

Jen, Carrie and Faith all exchanged quick glances. They knew Amber and Michael had been talking about having kids and they'd been anxious for an announcement.

Amber turned, and her eyebrows rose when she saw they were all staring at her. She laughed and said, "No, not yet. We're still in the talking stages. But when we do have kids, I'd sure want them to have the opportunity to be down here, like you guys have. It would be a shame if they couldn't."

"You're preaching to the choir here," Jen said as she put the last of the dishes away. "Tell grandpa. And Uncle Greg."

"I would if I could," Amber said. "But Grandpa's been pretty busy with Susanna, and I haven't seen Greg in ages."

Faith grabbed one of the apple pies, and Carrie picked up the plates and forks. "Well, Jen has some tricks up her sleeve, don't you, Jen? We're not going to let this happen."

Amber smiled at Jen, opened the door for Faith and Carrie, and followed them out onto the deck.

Jen paused for a moment, looking out the window again. She wasn't sure at all if she had any tricks left. And even if they did, would they work? She really didn't know anymore.

CHAPTER TWENTY-TWO

Michael set down his fork after the last bite of apple pie on his plate. "Amber says that dad's friend Joe is in town."

"True," Jen replied. "I really should have invited him. I guess I wasn't thinking. He's asked after you boys and would love to see you. Darn it."

Faith nudged Jen with her elbow and whispered, "Speak of the devil."

Jen looked where Faith was pointing to see Joe round the corner and look up at the house. Jen smiled—he was wearing his gondolier costume. One of their workers must have called out sick or something.

"Joe," she called and waved him over.

"Hi, everybody." Joe climbed the steps with his gondolier hat under his arm and a sheepish smile on his face.

"Good grief, Joe. You look the same as you did decades ago," Jen's father said as he shook Joe's hand. "Same outfit and everything."

Joe laughed. "Yeah, I guess so, Mr. Watson. I'm filling in at the gondolas. My dad passed away, and we're deciding what to do with the business."

"Good man. I say keep it. It's a goldmine, I bet, and looks like fun."

Jen reintroduced him to Michael.

"Wow," Joe said, looking from Jen to Michael and back again. "You sure look like your dad." His eyes clouded for a moment, and he shot another quick glance at Jen. She felt her heart tug at the same time, knowing that this would be difficult for him. For all of them.

"I'm so sorry I can't stay. I've got a reservation and I've got to get down to the dock. Jen, any chance we could schedule another get-together? Maybe in a few weeks? I'd love to catch up with everybody. Just kind of indisposed at the moment."

"We've got to get going, too," Michael said as he reached for Amber's hand. "But we'd love to take a rain check. Schedule something, though. Just let us know where and when, Mom."

"Great," Joe said as he shook Jen's dad's hand again and nodded at Susanna and the girls. "Count me in."

Joe headed down to the harbor along with Michael and Amber. After they'd gone, Jen looked up and down the street once more for Greg.

"Dad, are we going to talk about this or not? I know you got a price range that Dirk thought would be realistic for selling the house. And you said you and Greg have been talking about it."

Jen's dad sat down beside Susanna, who mercifully

had not joined in much conversation—so far. Unfortunately, it didn't last.

Susanna happily chimed in. "They have been talking about it. A lot. In fact, we cancelled a couple dinners because of it. I tell Jim, 'You don't need to be worrying about all of that old stuff. We have places to go, things to see.'"

Jen thought she actually heard Carrie and Faith gasp behind her. They were on the other side of the deck, pretending not to listen, but Jen had the same reaction.

Jen's dad shifted in his seat and rested his hand on Susanna's knee.

"Well, Susanna's not completely wrong. We have some trips planned, and I just don't want to worry about all this. I know you guys love the house, but I've had my fun here. I want to see some other places while I still have time. And Susanna and I mean to make it happen."

Jen's spoon dropped to the table with a thud. She couldn't believe what she was hearing. She shook her head and rallied.

"Okay. Greg and I will just take care of things. Just keep things the way they are. No huge repairs—or I'll figure out how to make that happen. Let's just not sell."

Jen's dad shook his head slowly and stood, reaching for Susanna's hand.

"I'm okay with whatever you decide to do. But that's a lot of money to just turn up your nose at, Jen. You need to think this through."

Jen had thought it through. More times than she could count. The memories—old and yet to come—

meant more to her than money. Allen had left her comfortable enough, and she still owned her other house. She could make it work.

Sure, things were lean, but she was safe. And if something happened to the beach house, she would never in a million years have the money to buy something different.

"I have thought it through, Dad. Hear me out."

"Honey, I have heard you out. And I've heard Greg out, more times than I wanted to."

"That's the truth," Susanna said with a giggle. "I told him just get rid of it. You don't need to worry about that stuff."

This time, Jen's dad actually steered Susanna toward the gate and pulled on his jacket. He gave her a bit of a stern look—one Jen knew well. She mouthed the word, "Sorry," and covered her mouth with her hand.

"I decided that this house is really your and Greg's inheritance anyway, from your mother's side of the family. Not mine to worry about anymore. So I had things changed. It belongs to you now, equally. You can decide what to do—the two of you together. And whatever you decide is fine by me. I know you'll make a great decision."

Jen was utterly speechless as her dad said his goodbyes to Faith and Carrie, who looked as shocked as she felt. He hustled Susanna out the gate and headed down the street, Susanna taking two steps to his every one to keep up.

"Well, that's quite a turn of events," Faith finally said as Jen's father turned the corner, looked back and waved.

"That is the understatement of the century."

"Is that a good thing or a bad thing?" Carrie asked.

"I can't imagine it's good," Faith said slowly. "Now you're stuck with just Greg."

Jen ran her hands through her hair. "And he won't even talk to me. But I guess now with Dad out of the mix, he'll have to. Whether he likes it or not."

CHAPTER TWENTY-THREE

Joe paused for a moment and watched Jen's son drive away. He could barely wrap his head around how much time had passed. He was over six feet tall, but when Joe looked at him, he saw him as a toddler. Even still.

He was strong and kind—he could tell. Allen would have been so proud.

He shook off the memories and headed down to the gondolier dock.

"Sorry to have to call you, Joe." Frank, a big, burly man his father's age, pointed to the gondola he'd be steering. "These young kids. I tell ya. Guess they had better things to do on a holiday."

Joe was no stranger to having better things to do than work a gondola. He'd done it all through high school and college, and he and Allen had been tempted to bail on work more times than he could count. But they never had. People made their reservations months in advance, and many were for special occasions. He'd never had the heart to disappoint them, which was why he was there now, holding onto the gondola as his clients stepped in.

He'd heard that it was a wedding proposal—from a soldier back from a tour for a brief time who'd wanted to do it on the Fourth especially. There was no way he was going to let him down, and he gave him a wink as the man helped his girlfriend into the gondola.

He had a special route he liked for these kinds of events—into the back, smaller bays with quiet houses and calmer water. He didn't talk much this trip, as the couple was chatting and looking at all the houses decorated for the holiday.

With a smile and a nod to the future groom—at least he hoped that was how it would turn out—he guided the gondola to a stop and waited, quietly, while the man proposed. He did his best not to listen and tried to distract himself counting how many of these scenes he'd witnessed over the years. In his life as an accountant, doing people's taxes had never been as rewarding, and he realized that he'd missed this. Being with people.

The pretty woman's tears and an excited screech let him know that the mission had been successful, and he turned the gondola back toward their pier. As they continued to chat and make plans, he looked around at the harbor. So much had changed. And then he thought of Michael's face, so much like Allen, and realized that some things hadn't changed at all.

CHAPTER TWENTY-FOUR

"All right, Greg. Dad told me that the house is yours and mine and you'd better call me back as soon as you can. It's time to have this out once and for all."

By the time Jen hung up, she was so mad she could spit.

Not only had Greg known about this change, but he had blown off coming down on purpose, so that her dad could break the news to her. She just knew it.

"What a coward," she said when she joined Faith and Carrie on the porch. The fireworks over the bay would be starting soon, and they had prime seats and a chilled bottle of wine.

Carrie rubbed her eyes and pulled her hair back into a ponytail. "I honestly don't recognize him anymore. He was always so nice when we were little. Remember that time he fixed your surfboard—before you gave it up? And he was always willing to go swim across the bay with us, and take us down to the water when our parents said we couldn't go alone. What happened to *that* big brother? He was so nice I was jealous I didn't have one."

"I didn't know him back then," Faith said. "I think I actually met him for the first time right after he got married to Sylvia. So that's not a Greg that I'm familiar with."

"Right," Jen added. "He really did change when he got married. Sylvia's okay. He just really changed. More worried about her family than ours. I never really understood it."

"Maybe they'll move to Angola or something," Faith said.

Jen laughed and leaned against the railing, noticing that it creaked when she did. That was new.

"Fat chance. They've got it made here. Her parents are loaded, and they have that beach house in Del Mar. Probably why he doesn't come here anymore."

"Well, I have been to their house once or twice. It's a lot—I guess 'newer' is the word I'd use." Carrie waved her arm out over the beach on one side of the house and over across the harbor on the other. "But she doesn't have this in Del Mar. There's nothing like it."

Jen shrugged. "I guess it matters what you care about. And he doesn't care about this at all."

"Can't you just say no?" Carrie asked.

Jen paced the deck, noticing every squeak. "I suppose technically I could, but how? Dad says he wants—no, needs—the money. I'm not sure I quite believe him, but it is quite a bit to pass up if Dirk's estimates are even close to correct. And it would take quite a bit to fix this up.

Some of this stuff is dangerous, especially if there were little kids around."

Carrie leaned against the railing and drew back as it moved with her. It wasn't supposed to. "Ugh, you're right. What a tough decision."

Faith squinted and pointed at one of the For Sale signs up the street. "Hey, he gave a pretty wide range for an estimated sale price, didn't he? If you listed it at the highest range or above, nobody would pay that much for a house in this kind of shape."

Jen stopped pacing and stared at Faith.

Faith held up both hands. "No offense intended. I love it. You know that. I just meant, what if things like this worked to our advantage?" She wiggled the hand rail to the steps for emphasis, and it moved more than it should. "I mean, if you set a really, really high price and sold 'as-is' I bet there'd be no takers."

Jen cocked her head and looked at some of the other houses around. None of them needed as much repair as theirs did. Maybe it wasn't such a bad idea after all.

"Yeah, and you know how you're supposed to keep the house cute and neat and tidy for when people come to look? I imagine that with no dishwasher, lots of dishes would pile up in the sink."

Carrie laughed. "Yes, and some of those fixes on the stairs could come loose. And Daisy here wouldn't mind knocking over a few more lamps."

Jen joined in. "Right. And all of that paneling I stuck back on is about to fall off anyway."

Faith looked around the house and nodded. "You guys, this might just work."

Jen's phone rang, and her heart leapt into her throat when she checked the caller ID. "It's Greg," she said, hopping up and walking down toward the beach.

"Hi, Greg," she said as she walked. "Thank you for calling me back. I was ready to drive down there and poke you in the eye."

Her brother was silent on the other end of the line for a moment. "I guess I'd deserve that. I'm sorry I wasn't there today."

"Why weren't you?" Jen tapped her foot on the boardwalk.

"Jen, I have something to tell you. I guess I wasn't brave enough to tell you face to face."

The tone in his voice made her shiver. He sounded sad and defeated. It wasn't something she'd heard often from him, but when she had, it had been something big.

"What is it, Greg?" she asked softly. "You can tell me."

He paused for a moment, and her heart tugged. "I need the money, Jen. I really do. My business is about to go under, and I don't know what to do."

Jen blinked a few times. Greg had an insurance business and had done pretty well. Apparently, not anymore.

She sat down on the bench on the boardwalk and looked out at the waves. She glanced back at the beach house, and Jen and Carrie turned away quickly, pretending they weren't wondering what was happening.

"What did Sylvia say?" she asked.

"That's the thing. I can't tell her."

Jen stood and began to pace. "Why not?"

"She's been after me to sell the business, retire. We want to travel, while we're still young enough. She's been bugging me to sell it for ages, before something happened. And now it's not worth a thing. She won't be very happy about that."

"Well, what will the money from the house do for you?"

"I could just let the business go. Pay the staff a severance and just retire."

For a moment, Jen felt sorry for him—until she had another thought. "Why don't you sell Sylvia's beach house? Why this one? It's all I have."

"You know that's not hers. It's her family's."

Her eyes narrowed. "So is this one, Greg. It's the family's. Not yours."

"I don't know what to say, Jen. I need your help. I don't feel very good about it, but I don't know what else to do."

Jen pinched the bridge of her nose. "Did you talk to Dad? He'd help you, I bet."

Greg sighed. "I can't. I don't want everybody to know that I failed. That I've lost the business. I was hoping to just tell everybody I retired."

"Greg, please just tell everybody. Dad would help. Sylvia would understand."

"Please, Jen. I can't. Things have been rocky enough over the years. I can't let everybody think I failed."

Jen sighed and closed her eyes. He was her only brother, and as much as they'd been out of touch, he'd done lots for her over the years. He was there for her when Allen died, and she should be there for him now.

"All right, Greg. I don't want to. This will break everybody's hearts, but okay."

Carrie and Jen both shook their heads slowly when Jen told them the news.

"I can't believe you said yes. He should just tell Sylvia. Ask your dad for some help. Anything but sell the house."

Jen nodded. "He should, but he won't. And I can't stand by and not help."

"Seriously?" Faith asked, her eyes wide and her hands on her hips.

"Seriously," Jen said, a slight smile crossing her lips. "If it doesn't sell, great. With the higher price, at least we'll be getting a bundle for it. But that doesn't mean I have to make it easy for him. If it doesn't sell, he'll have no choice but to tell Sylvia and my dad the truth."

Neither Carrie nor Faith looked very convinced that this was the right course of action, but Jen knew it was. There was nothing else she could do.

CHAPTER TWENTY-FIVE

I t turned out it was harder for Jen than Faith thought it would be to leave some of the rooms in the house in a bit of disarray. With Jen being a designer and all, it went against every fiber of her being, but Faith and Carrie were finally able to convince her that it was their best hope.

To make Jen feel a little better, she took down some of the throw pillows she'd been working on and set them out on the sofas. While the colors weren't exactly orange and avocado, she'd found some pretty Moroccan fabric before they'd headed down for the summer, and she'd brought her sewing machine.

The gold and orange fabric with reflective beading updated the look of the room just slightly—enough so that Jen was able to not be utterly embarrassed. Decorating was one thing—a house falling to pieces was quite another.

They'd all worked hard and sat on the deck after they were finished, toasting each other for a job well done.

"You think this might work?" Carrie had asked.

"If not, it won't be for a lack of trying," Jen said, looking up at the hole in the awning where they'd removed the duct tape that had been holding it together.

They watched the Fourth of July fireworks in silence, but Faith knew that the same thing was running through all of their minds. They just didn't want to say out loud that it might be the last time they'd watch from this deck.

Faith took a good look at the house on her way up to bed. They'd been so busy fixing things that she hadn't really noticed how many things were still not done. Everything was different now that they were going to stop moving down their fix-it list.

Jen and Carrie had mentioned more time to paddleboard or maybe even sail. But Faith had taken a look at her budget earlier in the day and was feeling a little anxious.

Her eyes fell on the job application that had been sitting on her dresser since they'd gone on the ferry over to the Island. She'd been intrigued by that shop that had all the pillows and trinkets from around the world. She'd gone back in when she noticed the "Now Hiring" sign on the door while Carrie was resting on the bench.

She'd chatted for a moment with the owner, Patti, and left with an application folded neatly in the pocket of her shorts. She hadn't thought she'd have time to do anything about it, but now, between the state of her budget and the change in plans for the beach house, she decided to check into it. She'd head out early the next morning and see what happened. It was worth a try, anyway.

The sound of the waves lulled her to sleep, and although the house was going to be for sale, she had a good feeling that maybe things might turn out okay after all. At least she hoped so.

CHAPTER TWENTY-SIX

"You got a what?" Jen asked Faith, her eyes wide open. "When—how—"

Faith draped her jacket over the kitchen stool. "I left early this morning while you were walking Daisy. I didn't want you to try to talk me out of it."

"Faith, if you wanted to get a job, I would support you one hundred percent. You know that."

Faith poured herself a cup of coffee and one for Jen. "I know, I know. It's probably more accurate that I didn't want to take the chance that I might talk myself out of it."

Daisy nudged her empty food bowl, and Jen realized she'd forgotten all about feeding the poor puppy. She was getting better by the day, though, and hadn't had any accidents in a while. She filled the food and water bowls before she even took a sip of her coffee.

"I think it's exciting. Tell me all about it."

"Well, my budget will think it's exciting, too. It could use some help, since I gave up that summer position. That's another reason I didn't mention it. I didn't want you to feel bad that I stayed to help with the house. But now that the plans have changed, I figured why not?"

"Right. I guess it'll all work out in the end. Where are you going to work?"

Faith rubbed her hands together. "That little shop on the Island. The one with the cool pillows that smell like incense. I met with the owner this morning, and she thinks it'll be a good fit. Just a few hours a week, but every little bit counts."

"It sure does," Jen said. "When do you start?"

"Not until next week. I thought maybe we could do some paddleboarding, maybe swim a little bit?"

"That sounds great," Jen said, her voice trailing off as a truck pulled up in front of the house and parked.

She and Faith grabbed their coffee mugs, opened the door for Daisy, and followed her out onto the porch.

"Mrs. Westland?" a young man asked as he glanced at a clipboard in his hand.

"Yes, that's me." Jen tried to stay calm as the young man nodded and reached into the back of his truck. He pulled out a big metal sign with Dirk Crabtree's picture and big red letters that read For Sale on it and looked around for a place to put it in the small courtyard. He moved toward her nana's rose bushes, and Jen jumped to her feet.

"Not there. Anywhere but there." Jen rushed down the deck stairs, Daisy close behind. She pointed to a corner by the garage. "You can put it there."

The young man pushed his baseball cap up on his forehead. "Mr. Crabtree always tells me to pick the place where people will see it best. I don't think that's—"

"I'll take that up with Mr. Crabtree. I'm the home-owner. Just put it there, like I said."

"Good call," Faith whispered loudly as he stuck the sign in the small patch of dirt by the garage.

The sign wasn't exactly invisible, but Jen figured not as many people would notice it there. As she turned back to the house, Mrs. Grover's curtain fell back into place.

It wouldn't be long before everybody on the block knew what was happening, and Jen's stomach dropped.

"Oh, Faith, this is just impossible. I can't believe it's even happening." Jen sat back down, and Daisy laid down on her feet as if in sympathy.

"I know, Jen. I can't believe it either. But we can still hope that nobody cares. I don't imagine other people think it's as awesome as we do, and you can kind of get a feel for the place just looking at the awning."

Jen smiled as she looked up at the blue-and-white striped awning with the big rip in it. It billowed in the breeze, and with the chipped paint on the window sills out in front and the wavering bannister, she knew it was true. She couldn't imagine anybody wanting to pay that much money for something that needed so much work. At least it was the only ace she had up her sleeve, and they were about to find how well it would work. Or if it would work at all.

CHAPTER TWENTY-SEVEN

"Wow, check out those guns."

"What?" Carrie shouted back from her paddleboard across the bit of water that was between them.

"Your arms. You're getting muscles. That's what they call it at the gym. Big guns. At least that's what the boys tell me," Jen said.

Jen and Carrie had been paddleboarding sometimes in the late afternoons for a couple of weeks, and Jen did have to admit that she was getting in better shape, too.

When they'd first started, she could barely stand up. Not that the paddle board wasn't stable—she was surprised at how stable they actually were. And once she'd gotten the courage to stand up right away, it had been pretty easy. So after Carrie got off work, she'd come down to the house and they paddled around in the bay. Faith joined them most days, but today she was at work.

They'd made a pact that by the end of the summer,

they'd make it all the way around. That was a pretty big target and it would take hours, but they were determined.

Jen had put on loads of sunscreen and had on a long-sleeved rash guard over her bathing suit. She couldn't help but laugh as she looked back at her friend—Carrie was Carrie. And Carrie had on a rash guard, flowered diving pants and a big, floppy neon-yellow hat. None of it matched, but Jen didn't mind. She was easy to spot when they got separated.

"How're the fundraiser plans going? I feel like I haven't been helping much. I need to ask Joe when would be a good time to go through Mr. Russo's things. I honestly hope we're going to find some treasures that Mrs. Russo is willing to part with. That would be great, wouldn't it?"

Carrie nodded and pointed out a little back canal that she wanted to go down. Some of the biggest houses in Newport were on these smaller canals, and they always liked to see what the neighbors were up to. Jen was a hundred percent positive that there wouldn't be any with ripped awnings and chipped paint. Not in this part of town.

"I haven't talked to Dirk in a while either. That would be great. I figured he'd call me if he needed help. And he hasn't. I already gave him the donations that we got right in the beginning."

"Oh, good. I haven't talked to him either. Since that first week, nobody's come to see the house, which is fine by me. I don't know. Maybe I should check in with him."

"Sounds like we both should," Carrie said as they glided past some of the biggest houses in Newport.

Jen had always been in awe of these houses since she was a little kid. She even knew which one had been John Wayne's. And nothing was different now. Some of them looked like castles that twenty people could live in. She'd been in some over the years, and the insides were as beautiful as the outsides. And at Christmastime, they were even more spectacular, all lit up with Christmas scenes ready for the boat parade.

Now, though, in the middle of summer, the palm trees swayed lightly in the breeze, and they looked elegant and peaceful.

"I'm ready to sit on the deck for a bit. How about you?"

"No argument from me. My muscles hurt. I really am too old for this."

Carrie pulled her paddle board up on the beach, inching it up the sand. "Your arms tell a different story, my friend," she said with a laugh.

"Well, I guess I should do whatever I can to keep the years at bay. But I am definitely tired and ready for a glass of wine."

They stowed the paddle boards in the garage and went around to the deck.

"Well, speak of the devil," Carrie whispered to Jen.

"Hello," Dirk Crabtree said from the deck. "Exactly the two ladies I was looking for. I hope you don't mind that I waited for a bit to see if you might come back, Jen. I needed to talk to Miss White, also, so this is just a bonus."

Carrie shot him a dirty look, but he seemed nice enough, and it was hard to hate him, even though he was the enemy. Maybe not the enemy for the fundraiser but the enemy trying to sell Jen's beach house. It was a little confusing, to be honest, to know whether to like him or hate him.

"Well, I've been completely avoiding you," Jen said as she smiled and sat behind him. "I figure if I avoid you, I don't have to talk about selling the house, and I can just pretend it isn't happening."

Dirk sat down beside her and shook his head. "No can do, ma'am. You guys hired me to do a job, and I aim to do it. Your brother calls me almost every day to check whether or not there's been any action."

"I bet he does," Jen said under her breath.

Dirk shuffled some papers and didn't notice. He just kept talking. "Potential buyers don't seem to be noticing the house. I don't think it's the price, although we did go on the high end. But people should still be looking."

He looked past Jen, over her shoulder and raised his eyebrows. "Or it could be the sign placement. You can barely see it."

Jen lifted her chin in defiance. "I think it's perfect. It wasn't going to go in my nana's roses. No way."

"Okay, fine. I have another idea, anyway. I want to have an open house. I'll advertise in the Daily Pilot and put it online so all the realtors see. It's a good way to get traffic through the house, especially during the summer."

Carrie took a quick look at Jen, and knew she was about to say something she might regret later.

"That'll be great, Dirk. What time?"

"Noon to three works best around here. Next Sunday.

You guys will need to vacate, but I will be here the whole time."

"Good," Carrie said, glancing again at Jen whose face was redder than she'd ever seen it.

"And Carrie, maybe you and I can get together afterward and talk fundraiser. I have some big donations, and we can talk process. You know, who's going to emcee, how it's going to run, all that. It's only six weeks away. Clock's ticking." Dirk headed down the stairs and over to his SUV. "Want to meet at the Lighthouse Café after the open house? Around four?"

"Sure," Carrie said and gave him a half-hearted wave as he headed down the street.

———

"Did I hear him say 'open house'?" Faith opened the gate to the courtyard and gave Daisy a nice, long pat as she looked from Jen to Carrie.

The lump in her throat softened, and Jen found her voice.

"Yes. This Sunday?"

"Oh, wow," Faith said, sitting down slowly with Daisy at her knee. "That's soon."

"It sure is." Jen leaned forward, her elbows on her knees and dropped her head in her hands.

Carrie draped her arm around her friend and glanced at Faith. "Jen, nobody's coming to look at it. An open house won't be any different, you think?"

"I don't know. Usually the realtors make cookies and

stuff like that. People come just to look. It feels like we're being invaded."

Faith leaned forward, her hand on Jen's arm. "People may come and look, but that doesn't mean they're serious buyers. Or people with enough money to buy it. It might be all right."

Jen leaned back in her seat and squeezed her friends' hands. "Thanks for trying to make me feel better. I guess it just is what it is."

"Yeah. Darn Greg," Carrie said.

"Right. Darn Greg," Faith echoed, and Jen cracked a bit of a smile.

"Yep, all Greg's fault. Well, he'll be sorry."

"He will?" Faith asked. "I don't know. With all that money and Sylvia happy, won't he be happy too?"

"I know I said yes to this, but I hope not. I intend to make his life miserable from here on out," Jen said, and they all three laughed.

"Good. He deserves it."

They looked out at the waves as Daisy's tail beat a steady rhythm against the worn wood of the deck.

"I guess I should take her for a walk."

"We'll go with you," Carrie said, standing.

"I think I'd like to go alone, if you don't mind. I need to get used to this idea of all those strangers in Nana's house. I'll be right back."

"Right in time for happy hour," Faith said with a very bright smile, Jen noticed. She knew her friends felt awful about all of this, too, but she needed a little time to process.

What sounded like a cat fight bristled in the palm tree at the end of the walkway.

"Looks like the baby herons are at it again," Carrie said, reaching for the binoculars. "They're getting bigger already. Time's flying. We'll keep an eye on them while you're gone. I'd say we'd start dinner, but that wouldn't help you much."

Jen laughed, feeling a little lighter already. Whatever was going to happen was going to happen, so she might as well make the best of it. "Perfect. Just wait for me. I'll be right back." Jen clipped the leash to Daisy's collar and opened the gate.

Daisy didn't make her usual beeline for the water and instead headed north. Jen knew why when she heard Boris barking from up the boardwalk.

She arrived at Joe's house and the dogs tumbled together in the courtyard, acting like they hadn't seen each other in years.

"It's fun to watch them play, isn't it?" Joe said as he stepped out from the house, the wooden screen door flapping closed behind him.

"Definitely. Makes me happy."

Joe cocked his head and looked more closely at her. "You look like you could use some cheering up, actually. What's wrong?"

Jen shared the recent developments about the open house, and he shook his head when she'd finished.

"Oh, man, that's too bad. But like the girls said, it doesn't really mean much. They're usually just random people wanting to take a look inside. That's all."

Jen nodded half-heartedly. "I know. I just don't want to watch."

"Don't blame you. Hey, why don't you come by while it's going on, and we can go through my dad's stuff. Good a time as any. I bet Carrie's ready for some more donations. The fundraiser's not that far off."

Jen looked up to the second floor of Joe's house, at the window into his dad's room, and wondered what they might find.

"Sure, that'd be great. I needed to vacate anyway, and it'll get that task knocked off my list."

"Perfect," Joe said. "Oh, and before you come over, make sure you steam some broccoli or cabbage or something so the whole house smells. Even if the realtor brings cookies, it won't help. I hate broccoli. That'd be it for me."

Jen laughed with her full belly this time. "That's a great idea. I'll do it. At least it's something, and I won't feel so helpless."

"There you go. It's a plan. See you on Sunday, but don't bring any broccoli over here, please."

Jen grabbed Daisy's leash and headed back to the house, a smile still on her face. It may not be much, but it was something she *could* do.

CHAPTER TWENTY-EIGHT

No amount of deep breaths Jen could take calmed her nerves. She'd re-arranged the living room furniture at least three times in the past few days and would have again if Faith hadn't finally balked and said no.

"Nothing's going to make a difference. If they like it, they like it," Faith said when she went on strike. "If you're nervous, let's do something else instead. I've been sewing pillows when I'm not at work to keep my mind off it."

Jen had finally taken her friend's advice, and they'd helped time pass by making pillows. For what, they didn't know, but Faith had been inspired by the pretty pillows at her work. They'd gone to an eclectic fabric store and gotten some pretty prints and spent some evenings at the sewing machine, chatting and sewing like they'd been doing for years.

"At least Maggy didn't have to go. Remember when we'd bribe her with McDonald's French fries to go with us?"

"Good grief, yes. She still talks about it. Describes it as sheer torture."

"Well, we did spend quite a bit of time in fabric stores, that's for sure."

Now, Jen couldn't decide which of the pillows they'd made to leave on the sofa. They were almost too pretty, and she really didn't want to make the room look too nice.

She peeked out the window as Dirk parked in front and groaned.

"Here we go," she said to Faith.

"It smells like broccoli in here," Dirk said as soon as he came through the door, narrowing his eyes at Jen.

Faith coughed a little too loudly, and Jen shrugged. "We had some for dinner last night."

"Uh-huh," he said as he laid out his sign-in clipboard and brochures. "Smells very recent. You sure it wasn't for breakfast? If I'd known you were going to do that I'd have brought cookie dough to put in the oven."

"That would be an interesting combination," Jen said as she reached for Daisy's leash. "You have my number if you need me, right?"

"I do. I hope everything goes well, and I'll let you know. I'm meeting Carrie afterward. Why don't you join us? We'll be talking fundraiser, but I can let you know how the open house went, too."

As much as Jen didn't think she wanted to know how it went, she knew by then she'd be curious. At least curious enough to hope it went badly and then she could rest easier.

"Okay, I will."

"Deal. Lighthouse Café at four."

Faith's eyes brightened. She was always game for a restaurant night out. "Oh, I love the Lighthouse. Haven't been yet this summer. How did we forget that?"

"We've been busy," Jen said. "Why don't you come, too? Meet us there after work."

"Perfect. See you then," Faith said with a wave as she headed toward the ferry.

Jen grabbed the bag of muffins she'd made for Mrs. Grover before she left. She nodded goodbye to Dirk and purposefully did not wish him good luck. She and Daisy headed up the boardwalk to Joe's house, and she vowed just not to think about it for about it anymore.

"Hi," Joe said as she climbed the steps to the porch. "You all right?"

"Yeah, I guess. I'm fine. I did the broccoli thing."

Joe laughed and slapped his thigh. "I was just kidding. Should have known you'd probably do it. Gotta watch what I say. I'd forgotten about your tendency for mischief."

"Who? Me?" Jen batted her eyelashes at him with a feigned look of shock. They'd all been mischievous when they were younger. Joe as much as anybody.

"I don't think it's going to work, though. Dirk was opening all the windows when I left."

"Broccoli lingers for weeks."

"Weeks?"

"Well, maybe not weeks but too long."

"Pssst," Carrie whispered. "Do you have the goods?"

"Why are you whispering?" Jen asked as she handed the muffins to Carrie.

"I don't know. I just thought spies should whisper." Carrie took the bag and saluted. "I'll report back this afternoon, Chief," she said before she headed toward Mrs. Grover's house.

"What was that all about?" Joe asked as he led her up the stairs and down the hallway to his dad's room.

Jen really didn't want Joe to know what lengths they were going to in addition to the broccoli. Not yet, anyway. "Oh, nothing. I'll fill you in later. Where's your mom?"

"At church. They have a community lunch for anyone who wants to stay afterward, and she's cooking. She'll be back later."

Joe opened the door to the room and peeked his head in, looking back at her with his eyebrows raised.

"We're going to have to move some things aside to get in here."

Jen nodded and squeezed her way into the room after Joe.

"Wow. This is a lot of stuff," she said, looking around at the room.

The walls were covered with shelves, and the shelves were full of figurines. A table in the middle of the floor held a working model train with the most realistic additions Jen had ever seen to one.

"Wow, that looks real. Those mountains, and that lake —that had to have taken forever to do."

Joe nodded slowly. "It's an exact replica of the part of Italy my dad grew up in."

"You don't want to part with that, do you?"

Joe shrugged. "I never had kids. If I had a son, I'd want to give it to him, I suppose."

"Oh, Michael and Max loved model trains when they were little. I was always sorry that Allen wasn't around to make one for them."

"Well, I think we should save that, then, and see if one of the boys wants it. They may want it for their kids. Besides, my dad loved Allen like a son and would like that very much, I'm sure."

"That's very sweet. We need to invite Michael and Amber out so we can all catch up. I forgot all about it."

"Me, too. How about next weekend? I think I'm fully staffed for the rest of the summer. Shouldn't have to pull any gondola shifts."

Jen laughed. "Deal. I'll call them tomorrow and see what I can do."

Jen rested her hands on her hips as she turned in a full circle and looked at the rest of the things stuffed in the very small room. From posters on the wall to a glass-lidded tray of Mickey Mouse watches, most things seemed to be Disney-related.

"So. This is really amazing. I don't remember so many Disney things when we snuck in here. I think we were just looking at the train. What's the deal?"

Joe laughed and shook his head. "Have I got a story for you."

CHAPTER TWENTY-NINE

"Mrs. Grover?" Carrie said as she knocked on Jen's neighbor's door. She hadn't seen the woman in years—at least not more than her nose against the window as the curtains twitched. But the idea had struck her that it was the perfect place to spy on the open house, and when Jen had agreed to the plan, they knew that Nana's muffins would be the key.

"Mrs. Grover, are you there?" Carrie knocked one more time and finally, the older woman opened the door. Just a crack, but she did.

"Hello, Carrie. I haven't seen you in ages." Mrs. Grover opened the door a little bit more, but squinted and looked from Carrie's face to the bag and back up again.

"Hi, Mrs. Grover. I was wondering if I could come in for a minute. I brought you something. Muffins from Nana. Well, not Nana. Jen made them. But Nana's recipe."

She held out the bag, and Mrs. Grover's eyes lit up. She opened the door wide, beckoning for her to come in.

"How lovely. Would you like to stay for tea?"

Carrie breathed a sigh of relief and looked out the window, choosing the best seat to watch from.

"I'd love to, Mrs. Grover."

She settled on the settee nearest the window and opened the curtains. Mrs. Grover put a kettle on and Carrie leaned forward, watching people climb the steps of Jen's house. She frowned when Dirk welcomed them with a smile and a handshake.

Utensils clinked in the kitchen, and eventually Mrs. Grover appeared with a plate of muffins and a pot of tea. She'd used her best silver tea tray, and the small pot with sugar and the little pitcher with tea matched perfectly.

She set the tray on a lace doily that covered the coffee table, and Carrie thought of Nana.

"I'm so glad for the company, and it was so sweet of you to bring over some muffins. I've missed them sorely."

"I bet. They're delicious," Carrie said, craning her neck to see over Mrs. Grover's shoulder. She sighed as another young family came to the house, walking all around the deck.

"And I've missed my friend, too," Mrs. Grover added in a much more quiet voice.

Carrie paused, her teacup halfway to her mouth, and looked more closely at Mrs. Grover. Jen's nana and Mrs. Grover had been close friends. They'd walked together every day, and Carrie was suddenly struck with what a shock it must have been for Mrs. Grover to have suddenly lost her best friend. If something happened to either Faith or Jen, she didn't know what she would do, and a wave of understanding washed over her.

She spent the next few hours filling Mrs. Grover in on what was happening, her heart light at giving the older woman something to talk about. Together, they watched through the window, and when it was all over, Carrie gave Mrs. Grover a very sincere hug.

"Thank you for spending your afternoon with me, and letting me be a spy."

Mrs. Grover waved her hand. "Think nothing of it. I enjoyed your company, and it's not as if I'm a novice at it."

She giggled and covered her hand with her mouth, and Carrie smiled as she left.

Carrie glanced at her watch and knew she'd have to hurry to get to the restaurant. She'd stayed a while after Dirk had locked the house and left, and she'd need to step it up.

He waved her over from the upper deck of the Lighthouse Café. The replica of an old lighthouse had been beautifully designed. A circle of mirrors with lights behind them spun at the very top of the tall ceiling, and it was one of Carrie's favorite places, new as it was.

"Hi," he said as she slipped into a chair at the table set for five. The others would be along shortly.

"Hello. How'd it go today?"

"Ah, not that interested in the fundraiser, eh?"

Carrie fiddled with her napkin and then set it in her lap. The waiter asked for her drink order, noting that it was happy hour. She ordered a chardonnay—and one for

Carrie and Faith. She knew they'd be as nervous as she was.

"I'm definitely interested in the fundraiser, but I am more interested at this moment in the open house."

"Well—" Dirk started, "Don't you think we should wait for Jen? I don't want to tell the story twice."

"Oh, jeez," Carrie groaned. "Okay. Fine. So, Jen was going to see our friend Joe today about some donations. His late father had quite a Disney collection, and I think we'll get a big donation from that."

Dirk set his menu on his plate. "That'll be great. They always get high dollar."

Carrie nodded. "Good, then. And I already gave you the other donations we've received. How have you done?"

Dirk leaned back in his chair, his fingers intertwined behind his head. He grinned like the Cheshire Cat and Carrie leaned forward, wondering what the donation was.

"I got a trip for two to Hawaii. A week's timeshare, and an airline donated, too. Free tickets."

Carrie raised her eyebrows and slow-clapped. "Nice. Very nice."

Dirk nodded. "Thank you. I hope to get a pretty good sum for it at the auction. The children's wing really needs this."

"I know," Carrie said. "It feels good to help. Speaking of the auction, how does that work?"

"Well, we need an auctioneer. Your mother said you might be interested."

Carrie held her palms out toward Dirk. "No, no, no. I told her no funny business. I would collect donations, and that was it. And come to the event, of course."

Dirk speared a shrimp with his fork—an appetizer he'd ordered with drinks—and dipped it into the spicy cocktail sauce.

"I thought you might say that. What if we just stick with a silent auction? You know, the kind where people bid on paper. Much easier that way."

"Great. That works for me. All the preparation in that is in advance, and we can just monitor it as we go. We'll need an announcer for the winners, though," Carrie said as she reached for a shrimp. They were cold and sweet, almost like lobster. The menu said they were from the Sea of Cortez in Mexico—the best around.

"Perfect. I'll take care of it. But the fundraiser's only a month away. I think we ought to meet more regularly, don't you? I mean, we still need to coordinate all of these baskets and things. Get them wrapped up."

Carrie swizzled another shrimp in the spicy cocktail sauce. "So, you won't tell me anything about the open house?"

Dirk laughed and shook his head. "No. You'll just have to wait."

Carrie leaned over toward the floor-to-ceiling window and sighed with relief as she saw Joe and Jen heading for the door. She didn't think she could wait any longer.

CHAPTER THIRTY

J oe picked up a small figurine off one of the shelves and held it out to Jen.

"I didn't even know why until I was older. Every time I asked, he'd just smile and shake his head."

"Really? Did you guys go there a lot when you were kids?"

Joe picked up stack of postcards, each in a cellophane case, and flipped through them.

"No, not really. I knew that my dad had worked there at one time. He was trained as an electrician and worked there when they were building the original park. It went up in stages, and he worked on lots of different things. But the one he enjoyed working on best was It's a Small World.

"Oh, the one where you go through on a boat and all the little kids from around the world sing?"

Joe nodded and put the postcards back on the shelf.

"Yep, that one. Said it reminded him of the places he wanted to visit."

Jen picked up a gondolier figurine from one of the shelves. "Like this?"

Joe sat down on a folding chair by the train set and moved the engine forward a little bit, then rested his elbows on his knees.

"Believe it or not, he said that's where he got the idea to start the gondola company. He'd married my mom, had me, they'd moved here, and she loved to cook. He said it was one way he could bring Italy to California. Or something like that."

"It certainly turned out well. You guys have the best business in town."

"I guess so. I never really appreciated it until recently, when I came back and saw how much people love it. It's kind of cheesy, Italian gondoliers in California, but if you could see how happy these people are, you'd know what I mean."

"Oh, I've seen it. People love it."

Joe looked out the window and waved. "Ma's home." He turned back to Jen and held his arms wide at all the stuff in the room. "They do love it. And it's done really well for us. My parents loved doing it, so—I just think he was grateful to Mr. Disney for the idea."

Daisy and Boris nudged the door open with their noses and took position under the train table. Joe reached down and rubbed them both behind the ears, their tails thumping furiously on the carpet.

"That's a very sweet story."

"My Gino was a very sweet man," Joe's mom said when she popped her head into the room. "How are you two doing?"

Jen smiled and nodded at Mrs. Russo. "We're doing fine, I think, Mrs. Russo. Not sure where to start, really."

Joe stood gestured again at the full room. "There's so much in here, Ma. What are you thinking?"

Mrs. Russo gripped a tissue in her hands and stepped gingerly into the room. She dabbed a cheek as she looked around.

"Your father loved all of this, and I know other people would, too. But I will tell you, after decades sitting outside while he sat in here and searched the internet for collectors' items, my suggestion would be to just focus on one thing."

She turned to the shelves on the wall and picked up the figurine of the child dressed as a gondolier and one of a girl from Africa. "These meant the world to him. And he searched high and low for them. If the money is going to the children's wing at the hospital, he'd want you to take them and auction them off to the highest bidder."

Joe ran his hand through his hair and shook his head. "I don't know, Ma. Would anybody want them?"

Mrs. Russo raised an eyebrow and glanced at Jen. "They might if you can find all of the figurines from all of the countries on the ride. That's what your father was hunting for. I never knew for sure if he'd been successful. But if he was, it could be worth quite a pretty penny. And it would mean the world to him if it helped some kids."

"Let me get my laptop," Joe said as he followed his

mother out the door. "I don't even know what that is or what it means. But I bet we can find out."

Joe and Jen spent the afternoon researching the original ride and all the souvenirs that had been sold from that time. They hunted on shelves, in boxes, under tables and in the closet.

"I think—do we have them all?" Joe finally said, stunned that his father had collected so many.

Jen plopped down on the chair by the model train and looked at the notepad with her list. "I think we do."

"Well, I guess the next step is to try to find out how much it's worth as a collection. Ma wants to donate it, so that's a done deal. But I hope the auction will fetch a fair price."

"I bet it will. We just need to advertise it a little bit. Even though the auction is local, this one puts out a glossy brochure and spreads it far and wide so that people from other places can donate. We might really have something here."

Joe whistled softly. "Wouldn't that be something?"

Jen rested her hand on his shoulder. "It sure would. Quite a gift."

Joe rested his hand on hers. "My father would be so proud. Thanks for your help. Maybe you could come back and help me wrap them up sometime?"

"I'd be honored," Jen said. She glanced at her watch and took in a sharp breath. "I think we're supposed to meet those guys at the Lighthouse Café. The open house will be over by now. I wonder what happened. How it went."

Joe lifted Jen's chin, and their eyes met. He knew she'd

been nervous about it, but the time had flown by as they went through the figurines. He was glad he could give her a bit of respite from her worry, and he wanted to comfort her now. Even if he wasn't sure how things would turn out.

"Whatever happens, it'll be okay, Jen."

CHAPTER THIRTY-ONE

M rs. Russo wished Jen good luck as Joe kissed his mother on the cheek and they set out for the Lighthouse Café. She'd happily agreed to watch the dogs while they were gone.

"I have some nice leftover roast for them. They'll be happy. I promise. You two scoot."

Jen gave her a grateful smile and told Daisy she wouldn't be long, but it was clear that Daisy didn't care one whit as she wrestled with Boris in the courtyard.

It was a short walk to the Lighthouse Café but Jen was late—and more than a little anxious. She glanced at her watch a couple of times, and Joe grabbed her hand and picked up the pace.

"What's the worst that could happen?" he asked as they carefully crossed Newport Boulevard and got closer to the building designed like an authentic lighthouse.

"Oh, I don't know. Somebody liked it? Wants to buy it?"

Joe laughed and squeezed Jen's hand. "Well, yes, I

know that. You agreed to this possibility. But I'm still hoping it didn't happen. And won't."

Jen appreciated his optimism—she'd run out of her own.

"That was always a possibility. You picked a really high price, though, and it's unlikely. Think positive."

She was trying the best she could, but it wasn't working. When they made it to the Lighthouse Café, they met Faith in the lobby.

"Any news?" Faith asked. She was out of breath, too, and looked as anxious as Jen felt.

"No, none."

Joe told the hostess who they were meeting and she smiled, grabbed three menus and led them upstairs to the top floor of the lighthouse. It was one of Jen's favorite spots—but the sweeping view of the harbor and beach with boats bobbing in the afternoon sun didn't even catch her eye this time.

Jen introduced Joe to Dirk before she scooted into the chair Joe held out for her.

"Oh, I've seen your face around everywhere," Joe said to Dirk as he shook his hand. "You're big business. Signs all over. What's the word for that?"

"Ubiquitous," Jen chimed in and shrugged, smiling at Joe.

Dirk's smiled humbly, but what Joe said was true. You couldn't miss Dirk's signs all around Newport. And although she liked him, she wished her father had chosen someone much less competent.

Everyone at the table fell silent, and all eyes were on Dirk. He looked around the table, raising his eyebrows.

"How did it go?" Jen had no patience for any more pleasantries with so much at stake.

Dirk cleared his throat. "Well, I guess we'll get right to it."

"Thank you," Jen said.

"We had quite few guests. Lots of them commented on the throw pillows on the couch, but I didn't know where you'd gotten them. Some came in for a quick moment, looked around and left. It was probably the broccoli."

Joe nudged her under the table with his knee. Jen looked down at her menu and tried not to smile.

"At any rate, there were several couples who lingered. One couple had two cute little girls, and they spent a fair amount of time upstairs on the top deck looking at the view," Dirk said.

"Well, that sounds okay. Not like people were streaming through and coming back a second time," Joe said brightly, and Jen knew he was trying to cheer her up. "That young couple with the little girls came back a second time, to get my card."

"Oh." Jen flashed a weak smile over at Faith, who'd rested her hand on her arm, and at Carrie, who looked concerned as well.

"They asked a few more questions but nothing major. Aside from that, it was a regular open house."

Jen pinched the bridge of her nose and tried to shake off the feeling of dread that had swept over her. There was nothing she could do about any of it right now, and the sweeping view of the harbor finally caught her attention.

"It really is beautiful here. You can see forever," she said absently.

Dirk turned to look out the windows and nodded. "Yes, it's lovely. That's what that one couple said about the view from your house. That it's beautiful and you can see forever."

That didn't exactly make Jen feel better, and she knew he was right. The beach house was one-of-a-kind. One that she wanted to keep.

They ordered appetizers and chatted about the fundraiser. Carrie filled them in on the plans while Dirk nodded and seemed to enjoy his fish tacos, and Carrie and Jen cleaned up every morsel of the grilled artichoke and garlic fries that they'd shared.

As the waitress cleared their empty plates, Dirk's phone rang. He excused himself and went out on the patio to answer the call. Jen couldn't keep her eyes off of him. He paced on the deck for a while, with an occasional glance back into the restaurant and then out to the sweeping view.

He ended the call and sat back down, his eyes trained on Jen.

"Is everything all right?" she asked, her hand to her chest. She didn't know why, but her Spidey senses were on high alert.

"Well, I guess it depends on who's asking."

Jen ran her sweaty palms over her jeans. "Me. I'm asking."

"Then I guess the answer would be no. It's not all right. You just got a verbal offer on your house. Full price. Cash."

CHAPTER THIRTY-TWO

J en had spent the past week intending to start packing things up at the beach house, but just hadn't been able to. Ever since Dirk had let her know that Greg was very happy with the offer—she'd had Dirk call, as she just couldn't do it—a dark cloud had fallen over the house. They walked Daisy, made dinner, and watched the sunset from the deck, but the joy had been sucked out of it.

"Maybe we should be making the most of it as it'll disappear soon." Faith had spent hours trying to cheer Jen up, but nothing was working.

They'd been collecting boxes and putting them in the studio, but they were all still empty. Any time Faith asked if she wanted help packing, all Jen could do was shake her head and take another walk around the living room.

"Hey, maybe we should look on the bright side." Faith grabbed her laptop and sat down beside Jen. She brought up Zillow and turned to her friend.

"Look, the house is going away, but you're going to

make a ton of money. Have you even thought about what you might do with it? What about looking for another beach house? One that would be just yours."

Jen hadn't thought about the money at all. It was the memories that she cared about, but Faith insisted so they took a look at other houses on the peninsula.

"Sorry about that," Faith said as she closed her computer. Even with half of the money from the house, Jen couldn't touch anything else that was remotely like what she had.

"Well, if it's any consolation, at least the new owners have little kids. They'll get to grow up here, on the beach and the bay, like our kids did."

It wasn't exactly enough to make her okay with the sale, but Jen was, in fact, happy that another family would be enjoying what she and her kids had. That lifted her heart a little bit.

Jen's phone rang, and she glanced over at it. Faith looked at the caller ID and held it out to Jen.

"It's Michael."

"Oh, thanks," Jen said as she answered the call. He always cheered her up—he'd tried even when she'd told him about the beach house sale.

"Hi, Mom," he said when she answered.

"Hi, Michael. It's nice to hear from you. How are you guys?"

"Good. Very good. We were wondering if we could call in that rain check and come down for Sunday dinner. I'd like to spend some time with you, and at the house. And I'd like to talk to Joe. I have some questions. About Dad."

"Oh?" Jen cocked her head and glanced at Faith, who was very obviously trying not to listen—not that Jen would have minded if she did.

"Yeah. We talked about it on the Fourth of July, remember?"

Jen did remember and thought it was a great idea. She just hadn't been thinking clearly enough to plan it.

"That sounds fun. I'll invite Joe and his mother— you'll love Mrs. Russo. And we'll see if Maggy can come up. And of course, Faith and Carrie will be here, too."

"Great," Michael said. He paused for a moment before he spoke again. "Mom, would you be willing to invite Grandpa and Uncle Greg? I'd like to see them, too."

Jen's first thought was, "Ugh. No." She hadn't forgiven either one of them yet and she really didn't want to see them. But her son never really asked her for anything—especially like this. And maybe since he was curious about his dad, he just wanted to talk a little history. And now would be the perfect time, while the beach house was in the family.

"Why not. We'll just have a goodbye party for the house," she said, keeping her voice lighter than she felt. She hated to be mopey, and her kids didn't need to see this, anyway. They'd dealt with enough already in their young lives.

"Thanks, Mom. We really appreciate it. What can we bring?"

Neither Amber nor Michael was a great cook, so she gave them their usual assignment.

"You're on drinks. And ice."

"Perfect," he said. "And Mom? I just wanted to say I love you. I know this is hard, but we'll be okay."

"I love you, too, son. And thanks for that. See you this weekend."

Jen set the phone down slowly on the table and glanced over at Faith.

"So we're having a party? With Greg and your dad, too?"

Jen nodded. "Yep. A goodbye party. Might as well shake this off and change the energy up around here. Give her a good send-off to her new owners."

"Whatever you say," Faith said, her voice filled with reservation.

"Right. Let's just do it. No telling if Greg will come, anyway. Let's just enjoy the last of our time here."

Jen crossed over to the window and leaned her head against the cool glass as the waves crashed against the shore. What was done was done, and she might as well make the best of it.

CHAPTER THIRTY-THREE

The flowers on the dining room table made all the difference in the world. Jen had cut them all from Nana's garden—all her favorites—and Faith had produced quite a lovely bouquet. They'd used one of Nana's old pitchers for a vase, and with her favorite Limoges, the table looked spectacular. It reminded Jen of holidays past, when they were all together, and she smiled at the warm fuzzies it gave her. If they were going to say goodbye to the house, it was going to be with a bang.

Jen, Faith and Carrie had been cooking for a couple of days—well, Jen had been and Faith and Carrie had been valiant helpers. They'd made Nana's favorites and a few new ones. Mrs. Russo was bringing her ricotta cheesecake and had promised that she would teach Jen how to make it when they had more time. Jen couldn't wait, and had decided that her best bet to make it through all this was to allow new things to come into her life as she said goodbye to the old familiar ones.

"Looks beautiful." Carrie nodded approvingly at the table. "Just like old times."

"Exactly," Jen said as she stirred the pot of chili that bubbled on the stove. "I think it's an appropriate farewell party, don't you?"

"Definitely." Faith came down the stairs, arms loaded with pillows. "We have to make sure to take these with us," she said while she set them out temporarily on the sofa and chairs.

"They're beautiful, you guys. You're really doing a good job. As nice as any in a store."

Faith flashed Carrie a smile at the compliment. "Thanks. I've been trying. I've even taken some to the store, as we seem to always run out of inventory. The owner's kind of—odd."

"Faith, can you grab Nana's blue bowl from the sideboard?"

Jen focused on dinner, as guests would be arriving any minute and she wanted to be able to talk to everyone. She turned down the burners and glanced around the kitchen. She nodded, untying Nana's apron and slipping it over her head.

"Love you, Nana," she whispered under her breath as she hung it on the hook where it had lived for decades. It was the one thing she'd planned to pack first when the time came.

"Hi, everybody," Carrie said as Michael, Amber, Jen's dad and Greg all arrived together. Jen peeked through the window and down the street looking for Sylvia, but she was nowhere to be found.

They sat in the living room, and while Michael and

Amber made sure everyone had their drink of choice, Jen, Faith and Carrie arranged the chips, salsa, guacamole and mini-burritos they'd made on the coffee table.

"Hello, Greg." Jen tried to keep her voice calm as she passed by her brother.

"Hi, Jen. Good to see you," he said as he reached for a chip. Jen mustered a smile for him, but still couldn't get over the sacrifice he expected from her about the beach house. She'd given up trying.

Jen welcomed Joe and Mrs. Russo, oohing and ahhing over the cheesecake. It looked divine, and she told Mrs. Russo she couldn't wait to try it.

"You'll never look at cheesecake the same way after," Mrs. Russo said.

Joe laughed. "She's telling the truth, I'm afraid." He crossed over to Michael and gave him a hearty hand-shake, and did the same with Jen's brother. The smiles all around warmed her heart, and she got Mrs. Russo seated by the window. Faith brought her a Chianti and Carrie, Faith and Amber chatted with her while the men, including Jen's dad, wandered around the living room looking at all the old family pictures.

"Is that you and my dad?" Michael asked. Joe smiled warmly, as if he had a secret in his heart.

"Yes. That's us in our gondolier uniforms one summer. Oh, and this one is when we sailed to Catalina for the first time."

"You sailed to Catalina? Just the two of you?" Michael asked, his smile wide.

Joe nodded somberly. "Yes. We were scared out of our

minds, but we made it. There and back," he said with a laugh. "Never did it again until we had a little bigger boat. My dad taught us how. Your dad was a great sailor."

Michael nodded slowly. "I didn't know that. Thank you."

Joe wrapped his arm around Michael's shoulders, squeezing a little, and Jen dabbed at her eye with a tissue. The boys had been so young when their father died, and they had to get right to the business of surviving. She probably should have talked more about Allen, but she just couldn't back then. And over time, they asked less and less. She was grateful that Joe could tell them stories now that even she didn't know.

"You're welcome. He was my best friend, and I loved him very much. I miss him."

Michael and Amber exchanged quick glances, and a smile spread across Amber's face. She nodded slowly, and Michael cleared his throat.

"Well, I suppose it's perfect timing that we're all here, and talking about my dad. It appears that I'm going to be a dad, too, and I'm afraid I'm going to need all the help I can get."

Jen, Carrie and Faith all gasped in unison and jumped up, rushing to hug Amber. Hearty handshakes and hugs enveloped Michael, too, and Jen finally had to reach for another tissue.

"Holy cow, Jen. You're going to be a grandmother." Faith wrapped her friend in a hug and held on tight. Carrie did the same and sighed deeply, her heart full and warm.

"Oh, I can't believe it," Jen said to Amber with a big

hug, and when she looked over at Michael, she paused for a moment.

His eyes caught hers, and he crossed the room, sweeping her up in a big hug.

"Oh, Michael, I can't wait. I'm thrilled. You're going to be a wonderful father," she said as she rested her palm on his cheek.

"And you're going to be the best grandma in the world, Mom."

Jen's heart tugged as she glanced at her grandma's apron, her roses, her china. She could only hope to be half as good a grandma as her own, but she was up to the challenge. New memories could be as good as old ones, she told herself, and she turned toward the room that was full of love and knew it would be true.

CHAPTER THIRTY-FOUR

The ricotta cheesecake melted in Jen's mouth, and she glanced over at Mrs. Russo with an appreciative smile. "Wow, you're right. That's the best I've ever tasted."

Mrs. Russo nodded approval, and Joe laughed.

"It sure is delicious, Mrs. Russo," Jen's dad said as his fork clanked on his empty plate.

Mrs. Russo shifted in her seat and patted the bun at the back of her neck. "Thank you all. I'm glad you enjoyed it."

Everyone started chattering again, looking at the scrapbooks she'd gotten out. Amber was particularly interested in the pictures of the boys when they were little —both Michael and Allen.

Jen sighed and looked toward the kitchen when the phone rang.

Dirk's name popped on the screen, and she figured she should answer. There were only a few more days during the inspection period, and he probably needed something done.

"Excuse me, everybody." She grabbed her phone and headed out onto the deck.

"Hi, Dirk," she said.

He responded with a hello that gave her pause. He'd been helpful and supportive, and she actually did like him. He didn't sound quite right now, though.

"You sitting down?"

She hesitated and looked around, her heart beating faster. "No. Should I be?"

She thought she heard him sigh. "Yeah, probably."

He plopped down on one of the deckchairs. "Jen, I have some news."

"Good or bad?" she asked.

He gave a half-hearted chuckle. "Same answer as last time. Depends on who's asking. But since it's you, I'll go ahead and say it's not news that I think you'll be happy about, I'm afraid."

She gripped the phone more tightly and waited. "Okay, shoot," she finally said.

He sighed again, and she held her breath. "I just got a call from the buyers. The inspection report came in with some very, very expensive repairs. New roof, some new flooring, drywall problems."

"None of that is news to me," she said. "Those are all things I'd planned to tackle. But we listed the house as-is, so it shouldn't be a financial issue, should it?"

Dirk cleared his throat. "No, no, that's not it. They knew there wouldn't be any money for repairs."

"Well, that's good, isn't it?"

"It might be under normal circumstances. Happens all the time in Newport. But when it does, people just tear the whole thing down. Start over. Build a new house."

Jen blinked fast several times, not sure what he was saying.

"What?"

"I'm sure you've seen all the new construction around you. There aren't many of the old original houses left. People buy them for tear-downs and start over. Surely you've seen some."

She stood and paced the deck, looking down the street. She could count at least five new houses being built where there were once smaller, quaint houses like her grandma's.

"Yes, I have, but surely nobody would want to do that to our place. I mean this house. They can't tear it down."

Dirk's voice softened. "I was hoping that wouldn't be the case, Jen, but it is. I just wanted to let you know. Now, I mean, during the inspection period when you could still back out. In another few days, it'll be too late. Signed, sealed and delivered."

She sat back down hard on the deck chair.

"I'm sorry, Jen. I really am. Let me know if I can help in any way."

"Thank you," she whispered before she ended the call. "I will."

Jen's mind was a blur, and she could barely catch her breath. She looked out over the courtyard, at Daisy lolling on the small patch that she'd claimed, at her grandmother's roses, at the paddle boards leaning against the garage. Then farther out to the harbor and in the other direction toward the beach. She leaned back and closed her eyes. The warm, salty air didn't reach to her bones this time, and all she felt was cold. Cold and empty.

"Jen? You out here?"

Jen took a deep breath at the sound of her brother's voice. Tearing down the house? That was something that had never, ever crossed her mind as a possibility. And now it was a reality.

She didn't want to talk to her brother or even see him —this was all his fault, after all.

"Yep, on the deck," she replied, leaning against the railing. The herons were making quite a fuss, and the babies they'd been watching grow all summer were learning to fly.

"What the heck is that?" Greg leaned on the railing next to Jen and pointed toward the palm tree.

Just as Jen opened her mouth to reply, one of the babies—very big now—took flight and headed down to the beach.

Greg whistled, and Jen handed him the binoculars. "Wow. That's really something. We never saw that when we were growing up."

"No, we didn't. We were lucky to watch them this summer."

Greg watched the blue herons for a little bit, then set the binoculars back on the railing. He leaned forward and down to Nana's garden. "She loved those roses, didn't she?"

Jen noticed that Mrs. Grover's curtain was twitching again, and Greg noticed it, too.

He pointed toward the neighbor's house and laughed. "Looks like some things never change."

"Until everything does," Jen said quietly. She couldn't help herself. Not only were they leaving, but the house they'd grown up loving wouldn't even exist soon.

Greg quickly glanced in her direction, a pained look on his face. "Jen, I couldn't help but overhear your conversation with Dirk. I never expected that the house would be torn down. I thought some other young, happy family would own it. Make their own memories."

Jen squared her shoulders. She hadn't had the chance to tell her brother what she really thought, and she wasn't going to waste it now.

"Not only will *no* family get to live in this house, but my grandchild won't. Not ever. You have a beach house in Del Mar. This is all I have."

Greg stiffened at her words. He shoved his hands in his pockets and looked down at his shoes, shifting from one foot to the other, like he did when he was a little boy and their dad was mad at him for something or other.

"I'm sorry, Jen," he finally said. "I tried to tell Sylvia. Tried to make myself call Dad. I—I tried."

Jen plopped down onto one of the deck chairs and crossed her arms.

"Well, you didn't try hard enough."

He shuffled his feet again. "Honestly, I thought you might need the money. You know, being a widow and all. I was trying to help."

She rolled her eyes, and he looked away. "Is that how

you make yourself feel better? I would have told you if I did. Allen didn't leave a ton of money, but I have the house he and I built. I've worked very hard. If you had asked me, I would have told you I wanted the memories here rather than the money. But you didn't. So please don't use that as an excuse for not being willing to ask for help. From someone besides me."

Greg looked out at the palm tree.

"I guess I just assumed. I thought I was taking the best care of all of us."

"No. And I miss you. I miss my old big brother who always looked out for me."

Jen stood and opened her arms for a hug. Greg looked down again but opened his arms and wrapped her in a bear hug.

Greg held her shoulders and searched her face. "I'm sorry, Jen. I've got to go."

He kissed her quickly on the cheek and headed down the stairs. She leaned over the railing and saw him walk quickly down the street to his car, his hands shoved in his pockets without even a backward glance.

She dropped her head into her hands for a moment and tried to collect her thoughts. She looked up to see her brother disappearing around the corner, leaving her to break the news to the family on her own.

CHAPTER THIRTY-FIVE

The pounding of the waves wasn't nearly as loud as the pounding in Jen's head. She'd had a good cry before falling asleep, and all night long she dreamt about the house—mostly that it was no longer there.

When she'd agreed to put the house up for sale, she'd been certain that it wouldn't sell for that price. At the open house, she'd almost had a moment of gratitude that the young couple had liked it so much and would be teaching their own kids to swim in the bay. As she replayed what Dirk had told her in her mind, she realized that they'd only talked about the view, the beach and the location—not the house. She'd been so hopeful that she'd just missed it.

She wandered downstairs into the kitchen and sat on the deck with her first cup of coffee. She hadn't even had the presence of mind to get out of her bathrobe, and Daisy was starting to pace, anxious about her walk.

Jen hadn't heard a peep from upstairs, imagining that

Faith was sleeping in after their late night. They'd finished the bottle of wine almost in shock. No one knew how to cheer anyone else up after the news, and Carrie had headed home with her head down.

She threw on some shorts and grabbed flip-flops, holding Daisy off as best she could. Grabbing the leash, she followed Daisy as she tugged Jen down to the waves.

Like clockwork, just as Daisy shook and sprayed Jen with a blast of water and sand, Boris barked, and Daisy was off like a shot again toward Joe's house.

"This is becoming a nice ritual," Joe said as he stood from the deck chair, his hands on his hips. "I like it."

Jen laughed and shook her head. "I had no idea I could run this fast. Thought those days were long gone."

Joe gestured to the chair beside him. "Have a seat. Catch your breath. We're not that old yet."

"If you guys think you're old, you've got another thing coming. Imagine having a son your age." Mrs. Russo swung through the screen door with a mug of coffee for Jen. She accepted it with a grateful nod.

Jen had never thought of it like that, but it made her smile, and her heart lifted when Joe winked at her.

"Oh, Ma, you love it, and you know it."

"True," the older woman said as she leaned back in her rocker on the deck. "How are you doing today, dear? That was quite a shock yesterday."

Jen took a sip of her coffee. Even Mrs. Russo's coffee was better than most.

"It was. I had a good cry last night and woke up with a pounding headache, but my run with Daisy seems to have blown it out."

Mrs. Russo patted her on the knee. "Did you think about trying to plead your case again with your brother? He seemed like his old self last night. Until he left suddenly. Maybe he'd be open to reconsidering?"

Jen shook her head. "I tried. He said he and his wife had made the decision, and that he'd thought he was doing the right thing."

Joe leaned forward, his elbows on his knees. "And you told him that he was wrong? That you wanted to keep the house?"

"I did," Jen said. "Then he just said he had to go. At least I got a hug out of it."

Joe lifted an eyebrow. "Well, I suppose that's better than a poke in the eye with a hot stick," he said, his voice tinged with sarcasm.

"Joey, stop." Mrs. Russo turned to Jen. "I know it means a lot for you to be here. Especially with the baby coming and all. Maybe you should try again."

"Right, Jen. You've told me how much you want your grandkids to have the same experiences we had. Isn't that worth fighting for? He can't sell it without you."

Jen pondered that for a moment. It was true. She had given in because her brother, who she truly cared about, had said it was important to him. But what about what was important to *her*? And it did seem that with Michael and Amber's news, things were different.

"I think Joey's right, Jen. Can't hurt to try. This is all new information. Sometimes it seems like some things never change, but in the blink of an eye, everything does."

Jen finished her coffee and set the mug on the table.

"You're right, Mrs. Russo. I'll call him. I'd never forgive myself if I didn't give it one more try."

She waved at them both as she reached for Daisy's leash and set out down the boardwalk back to her beach house.

CHAPTER THIRTY-SIX

Jen took three deep breaths as she and Daisy walked back to the house, then reached for her phone. She dialed Greg's number and paused in front of the house when he answered. She slipped Daisy inside the gate and paced back and forth as she talked.

"Hi, Greg. I just wanted to tell you one more time that I really don't want to sell the house."

"Jen—"

"Just let me finish," she said, looking up at the ripped awning that she loved. "I have so many memories here, and so do you. You guys have someplace where you take your grandkids to make sandcastles. I won't have that anymore. Don't you love doing that with your kids?"

"Jen—"

She couldn't stop now. She had to get it all out. "Nana and Mom would have wanted this, for it to stay in the family. I know Dad doesn't care at the moment—that Susanna thing—but if he were in his right mind he would. Michael and Max—and your kids, too—deserve to have what we had. Remember all the good times? We even learned how to swim here."

"Jen, I—"

"Let me finish. I would like you to reconsider. You are my big brother. You and Sylvia are well-off, but I'm not. Dad will help you with your business if you ask him. Heck, Sylvia's dad would, too. If we sell this house, I'll never have a beach house again in my entire life. And my kids won't either."

She ran out of breath and arguments at the exact same time.

"Are you finished?" Greg asked.

Jen sat down on one of the brick fence posts. "I think so."

Greg laughed, and she cocked her head. She hadn't expected that at all. In fact, she'd half expected he'd hang up on her, given how he'd been behaving lately.

"Sylvia and I had a long, long talk. I explained to her what happened. I told her Michael and Amber's news. It didn't hurt that we were in Del Mar at the time, and the kids were playing on the beach."

"See? That's what I meant."

"I know, I know. And she completely understood. Said we'd been married so long that she'd take the bad with the good. So if you want to stop the sale, we're all for it."

Jen stood up like a shot and gasped. Mrs. Grover's curtain twitched ,and she could see Faith poke her head out the screen door, a question in her eyes. Even Daisy turned to look at her.

"Are—are you kidding?"

Greg sighed. "No. Not kidding. And I'm sorry I couldn't do it earlier. I know you've been through a lot of worry. I'm truly sorry for that."

Jen stared at her phone for a few moments before she could even respond.

"I don't know what to say. Thank you, Greg. I'm very grateful. I don't know how to thank you."

"There's nothing to thank me for. Thank you for being willing to help me. I just—well, I did my best. But I'm doing better now."

"Okay. Does Dad know?"

"No, I wanted to tell you first. I was just going to call you when you called me. And if you really want to thank me, make me some of Nana's muffins. Sylvia and I both love them, but we don't have the recipe."

Jen laughed and gave a thumbs-up to Faith. Carrie rounded the corner, rushing over and asking Faith what was going on.

"Consider it done," she told Greg before ending the call.

"Did I hear that correctly?" Faith asked as Jen walked slowly up the steps.

Jen almost couldn't believe that *she'd* heard it correctly.

"Yes. He actually doesn't want to sell the house. I'm shocked."

Carrie gasped and gave Jen a hug, and Faith did next.

"That's fantastic," Carrie said. "Change of heart?"

Jen nodded. "Yes. I guess he talked to Sylvia, and they both agreed that they wanted it to stay in the family, too. I guess the plans to tear it down got to all of us."

"I say a celebration is in order," Faith said. "Have dinner on the deck, toast at sunset."

"Right. And it won't be our last but the first of a million more," Jen said, squeezing her friends' hands.

———

Dirk came over later in the afternoon with the paperwork to stop the sale. They all stood behind Jen as she signed and broke out in applause at the final signature.

Carrie popped a bottle of champagne and they all toasted as they watched the young man who'd come with Dirk take the sign out of the yard.

"I thought you might want that out right away," Dirk said as he lifted his champagne flute at the driver when he pulled away.

"Very much so. Thank you," Jen said.

"You're very welcome. This was a tough job. Being hired to sell a house and trying hard not to let it happen was a new challenge for me."

Carrie laughed and said, "Well, you were up to it. You didn't have to let Jen know that they were going to tear it down. Good thing you did."

Dirk closed his eyes. "It wasn't confidential information. Normally, I might not even know that a client cared about that one way or the other. Fortunately, in this case, I had inside information."

"Thank goodness," Faith said as she set out chips and salsa.

Jen let out a big sigh of relief. "I second that."

"I third it," Carrie added.

"Can I be the fourth?" Joe led Boris through the gate and let him off his leash.

Jen's heart lifted as he smiled at her, opening his arms for a hug. She'd called and let him know about the change of plans and invited him over for dinner. She'd invited Mrs. Russo as well, but she was going to play bingo and said the young people should have fun without her anyway.

"Please stay for dinner, Dirk. We have plenty."

Dirk nodded appreciatively and rubbed his belly. "Don't mind if I do. Not often I get a home-cooked meal. Besides, Betty White and I have a lot to get to. The fundraiser is in less than three weeks, and we're not ready."

Faith laughed. "Oh, wow, with all the commotion, I forgot all about that. I guess we'd better get on it."

"Perfect opportunity to plan," Jen said. "I'll go start on dinner. You guys start on the fundraiser."

Joe followed Jen into the kitchen. "Can I be of assistance? I know zip about fundraisers. And I like to cook."

"Good thing." Jen glanced out the window at Faith, Carrie and Dirk jabbering already over a notepad. "None of them do."

Jen reached for her grandmother's apron she'd worn all summer. Hands of Gold, it read. She ran her fingers over the frayed hem before she slipped it over her head, ready to make dinner for her friends.

"I'm sorry I don't have an extra apron for you. This is the only one I kept."

"I see why. It looks special."

"It is," Jen said. "Just like yours," she said, stifling a laugh.

"Don't worry. I brought my own. Ma said I might need it. And you know she's never wrong." Joe smiled and reached into his back pocket, pulling out his own apron— the one with the heart on the chest.

Jen was overcome with laughter, and her belly hurt by the time she stopped.

"Boy, I needed that. Been a long time."

"It has. And I love to see it."

Jen looked at him, feeling grateful. "Thank you. I really appreciate it."

"Good. Because I expect that it will be the first of many, many more."

As Joe began to chop the onions that Jen handed him, she paused for a moment, looking out at the roses. She ran her hands down the fabric of the worn apron and nodded.

"Don't worry, Nana. We're not going anywhere," Jen whispered.

L abor Day finally arrived, and the day broke breezy and beautiful. Faith and Jen were already dressed and ready, and Carrie would be over in a moment.

Jen fluffed the pillows on the new—well, new to her—couch that she'd found at a second-hand store. She pulled back the new curtains and breathed in the salty air.

"Those curtains turned out great," Faith said as she came down the stairs. "I love the new colors."

"Yep, I love them, too. Perfect with the pillows."

Jen and Faith had been sewing for weeks, and Jen would defy anyone to find a speck of orange or avocado remaining in the living room. They'd even found brown leather stools for the kitchen counter. Next on the list was taking off the paneling, but for now it looked like a different house.

Carrie honked, and they grabbed their purses and said goodbye to Daisy. The fundraiser was at the yacht club, and they'd been over earlier to set up the silent auction. The place looked beautiful, and everything was in order. All they had to do was meet Dirk, Joe and Mrs. Russo and enjoy the evening.

"You look fantastic," Jen said as they hopped in Carrie's convertible. Her dress was orange—which was expected—but it was a little softer and more subtle than what she usually wore.

As they pulled up to the yacht club, Jen spotted Joe and Mrs. Russo heading inside.

"Hey, look at that," Faith said, nudging Jen with her elbow. "He cleans up great. Nice suit."

Jen ignored her, and they met up with their friends when they entered the ballroom.

"You look beautiful, dear." Mrs. Russo leaned in and kissed Jen on the cheek. "You all do."

Dirk came over and smiled approvingly. "You guys did a fantastic job. People are bidding like crazy, and everything is perfectly organized."

The girls flashed each other thumbs-up signs and found their table.

"Nothing left to do but enjoy," Carrie said as they sat down.

Joe pulled out Jen's chair for her, and Jen saw Faith wink at Carrie. He offered to get drinks for everybody, and when they'd placed their orders and he headed to the bar, Mrs. Russo sighed.

"What is it, Mrs. Russo?" Jen asked, frowning.

"Oh, I just wish Joey's father was here. He would have been thrilled to see the figurine collection. I noticed how much it's going for when we walked by. The bids have lots of zeroes. He'd be so pleased."

"Wonderful," Carrie said. "That was the plan. The children's wing can use it."

Mrs. Russo nodded slowly. "That's wonderful."

Joe came back with the drinks and Jen took her glass of chardonnay from him. He gave his mother her Chianti, and Dirk followed behind with wine for Faith and Carrie. He started chatting about the fundraiser with them, pointing to the crowds of people around each auction item, and Jen was pleased that it looked like such a success.

Mrs. Russo took a sip of her wine and glanced over to the balcony that had a sweeping view of the bay.

"Oh, look. The sun's about to set. Looks like it's going to be a beauty."

Joe stood. "You want to go watch it, Ma?"

"Oh, no," she said. "But you two go ahead."

She smiled sweetly toward Jen, then looked at Joe.

Joe laughed and held his hand out for Jen. They strolled out onto the balcony and leaned against the railing. The sunset was, in fact, spectacular. Bright oranges, blues, reds—and it would only get better.

She glanced at Joe. She loved his smile. He looked down at her, and she looked away quickly, surprised that she'd noticed his soft lips.

"Looks like summer's almost over. Not such good weather after Labor Day," he said. "I've made a decision, though, and I wanted you to know."

"Oh?" she asked.

"Yeah. Ma and I have decided to keep the business, and I'll retire from my accounting firm. Working a gondola is a lot more fun than working spreadsheets."

Jen laughed, and the news warmed her heart. She wanted Joe to be happy. And she wanted to be happy herself.

"And you. Now that the house isn't up for sale, you can enjoy the rest of the summer."

Jen sighed and glanced at the sunset that was now turning into deep pinks and purples.

"I can't think of anything I'd rather do."

———

I hope you enjoyed *Newport Harbor House*! In the next book in the series, *Newport Beginnings*, the fundraiser turns out to be a disaster, and Carrie's life is about to be turned upside down.

Newport Beginnings

Have you read *As Deep as the Ocean* yet?

If you'd like to receive an email when my next book releases, please join my mailing list.

ABOUT THE AUTHOR

Cindy Nichols writes heartwarming stories interwoven with the bonds of friendship and family that combine what she loves most about women's fiction and romance.

Cindy lives in and loves everything about the southwest, from its deserts and mountains to the sea. She discovered her passion for writing after a twenty-year career in education. When she's not writing, she travels as much as she can with her children who, although adults, still need her no matter what they think.

Feel free to sign up for her list to hear about new releases as soon as they are available. Click here to sign up:

Cindy's Email List